RANSOMED

(anatomy of a refugee)

ESSENTIAL PROSE SERIES 163

Guernica Editions Inc. acknowledges the support
of the Canada Council for the Arts and the Ontario Arts Council.
The Ontario Arts Council is an agency of the Government of Ontario.
We acknowledge the financial support of the Government of Canada.

LAURA
SWART

RANSOMED

(anatomy of a refugee)

**GUERNICA
EDITIONS**

TORONTO · BUFFALO · LANCASTER (U.K.)
2019

Michael Mirolla, editor
Cover and interior design: Rafael Chimicatti
Guernica Editions Inc.
1569 Heritage Way, Oakville, (ON), Canada L6M 2Z7
2250 Military Road, Tonawanda, N.Y. 14150-6000 U.S.A.
www.guernicaeditions.com

Distributors:
University of Toronto Press Distribution,
5201 Dufferin Street, Toronto (ON), Canada M3H 5T8
Gazelle Book Services, White Cross Mills
High Town, Lancaster LA1 4XS U.K.

First edition.
Printed in Canada.

Legal Deposit – Third Quarter
Library of Congress Catalog Card Number: 2019930425
Library and Archives Canada Cataloguing in Publication
Title: Ransomed: (Anatomy of a refugee) / Laura Swart ;
Names: Swart, Laura, 1963- author.
Series: Essential prose series ; 163.
Description: Series statement: Essential prose series ; 163 |
Identifiers: Canadiana (print) 20190052333 | Canadiana (ebook)
20190052465 | ISBN 9781771833875
(softcover) | ISBN 9781771833882 (EPUB) |
ISBN 9781771833899 (Kindle)
Subjects: LCSH: Refugees—Canada—Interviews.
Classification: LCC HV640.4.C3 S93 2019 | DDC 305.9/069140971—dc23

anatomy
(late Middle English: from Old French anatomie
or late Latin anatomia, from Greek,
from ana-'up' + tomia 'cutting'; from temnein 'to cut').

Author's Note:
This book is based on true events.
Names, details, and scenes
have been changed to protect identities.

Contents

Act One: Passover

(PESACH) — NISAN (MARCH-APRIL)

Everything happens outside. There's a quarry. And a canopy. Guests sit in folding chairs on a small hill of grass, looking down at the canopy. Mason jars with white flowers hang by a wire from the aisle seats. A fiddler stands at the front, to the right of the canopy, playing Great Big Sea songs: *Mari Mac. It's the End of the World as We Know It. Lukey's Boat.*

Everyone waits. Time comes undone and then stops at precisely 3 pm: The groom has arrived. He comes up from the quarry like a column of smoke, his hair black like a raven. He waits, waits like a watchman, his eyes mounted like jewels. And then, everyone stands: The bride is at the crest of the hill. The aisle is narrow, a thin pathway through wooden chairs. She walks, close in. Her dress is not too white: It has a golden, paper-bag sheen, gathered up at the back into a silhouette. Her expression is layered—sheaths of fear with joy mixed in. She holds a thin alabaster jar of almond blossoms. She's walking on the grass, her dress a wide circle, and she's lovely. But she's not the main attraction.

The groom is.

His hair is shaved on the sides, swept up at the top into a wave held tight, and his face is round and bright. He shifts his weight from toe to toe, waiting for his bride, waiting for his bride. From somewhere behind him a shofar blows. It's coming from the fiddler: He has put his fiddle aside and taken up the shofar, lovely and curved and soft like orange needles on larch trees, and the sound spills out from the shofar's sleeve and races up the hill, and the people's hearts are moved like trees of a wood are moved by the wind.

She comes to him, and he misses everything else. He misses the rabbi's words and he misses the songs and he misses the blessings and the guests. He remembers later the wine glass. Stepping on it, crushing it like Solomon's Temple. He remembers the grapes, holding sweet nectar then letting go, water turning into wine. He remembers being hoisted up high in a chair, his guests dancing and shouting below.

He misses it all because he can only see his bride—her white dress mingling with the green grass and the brown earth, the edges turning yellow-green like a mountain lake cool in the morning with the breath of

God brooding on its surface and serrated peaks skirting its margins like pillars of a temple, their reflections heavy in the green lake, green because precious stones are on its floor, jasper and sapphire, agate and emerald. The groom thinks of these things as he watches his bride, watches the grass brush against the edges of her gown, staining it topaz.

But it took his bride a long time to come to this place, to come to this aisle and walk towards him. Because, you see, he is Jewish.

Act Two: Unleavened Bread
(CHAG HAMATZOT) — NISAN (MARCH-APRIL)

Think. Think of a camp. What immediately comes to mind? Nazi Germany, you say. Of course. Concave torsos and horse's teeth. Matted hair, fingernails thick like broken bottles. You have the picture, then. Now come back a little. Japanese internment camps in the Kootenays. Chinese building the Canadian railroad, living in boxcars and tents and later burrowing with the rats into dark tunnels and raising families there. Okay. Now come away, further. Think about camping as a child. Setting up, taking down. Deep woods. Coleman tents and lanterns, wieners sizzling in the fire. Tea steeping—or maybe those broken bottles again.

But think about this: What defines a camp? Isolation. Essentials. Deprivation, even. Think of the etymology of the word. Early 16th century French 'camp' or 'champ' from the Italian 'campo' and the Latin 'campus'—'level ground'—specifically referring to the Campus Martius in Rome, used for games, athletic practice, and military drills. Military drills. Now you're getting it.

Act Three: First Fruits

(YOM HABIKKURIM) — NISAN (MARCH-APRIL)

We meet in a house of sorts. A big house with little rooms that hold people. Orphans, widows, the disenfranchised—refugees, we call them. The house is like the osprey nests I see in the woods by the river. Ospreys allow songbirds to build homes on the lower level of their nests, providing them with security and protection from predators. The refugees live in the little rooms, which look like they belong in a nursing home: flat and hard and colourless. People go to nursing homes as a last stop before entering the next world, and I suppose it's the same for these refugees. They arrive intermittently in taxicabs sunken down with luggage: big families. They come mostly from Syria, Iraq, Eritrea, Burundi, South Sudan, and Congo and stay for six months. The house holds eight families. It is almost full now; there is room for one more family. They will learn English, learn the customs, find a home, find a job. They will be herded from doctor appointments to counsellors to food banks to bankers to bus depots to cell-phone kiosks to registrars. Interpreters working in the house, former refugees, help them with these things. And then they will all fly away, like a swell of waxwings.

We call our house The Booth. I don't live in the house. I live outside the city in a wildlife corridor. Close to the mountains, next to a quarry. I need the isolation. Sometimes at night I hear coyotes howling. I hear dogs barking, too. I can tell the difference. A bark has an abrupt beginning and end; it punctures the air, breaks it up into pieces. But a howl rides on the air. It is born on the air and dies with it. Sometimes a dog will escape from its yard and come upon a coyote, and I hear the desperate struggle and cackling and yelping in the dark and the inevitable silence that follows.

When you think of a quarry, the first thing you think about is a deep pit. Cutting into the rock to extract stone or coal or minerals. But the word *quarry* has other meanings. It comes from the Old French *cuiree*: 'the spoil,' and is influenced by *curer*—'to clean, disembowel.' From Latin come the connotations *corium*, 'hide,' and *corata*, 'entrails.' A quarry, ultimately, is anything that is chased in a hunt.

The refugees come to my English class every day, in the basement of The Booth. We sing. That's how I teach English: singing. Each song is a gift—a package of intonation, vocabulary, grammar, and syntax. I give them the package and they open it, learn the song. They don't understand the words, but that's not entirely important. They will understand later. Memorize now, understand later.

* * *

I'm in my classroom, waiting for the students. Chickadees gather outside on the window ledge eating the seeds I've put out for them. Chickadees are wild animals, of course. But they feed from your hand. They gather into residential flocks with strict dominance hierarchies, and I watch as subordinate birds cede their positions on the ledge to larger birds that fluff themselves out into little balls, lean into them, and emit crisp, bi-syllabic chirps.

Ahmed comes into the classroom. He is Syrian. His skin is textured like an overripe avocado and he has a slight hump between his shoulders, making his neck protrude like a bird's. I extend my hand, but he won't take it. He won't take my hand because I'm a woman.

"How do you think you'll survive here?" I say.

"Yes?"

"Forget it."

His wife comes in behind him. Her hijab is taut around her face. Thick, inky black. But her eyes are peridot green and her nose is thin and long like a sandpiper's beak. I try to coax a smile from her, but she's tired. Her hands are scarred. I want to ask, but I don't. I ask instead what her name is.

"Her name Mayada," Ahmed says.

I direct my attention to Mayada. "How many children do you have?"

Mayada looks to Ahmed. "Five children," he says.

The room starts to fill up. They come in clusters of families and cultures—residential flocks: Tribes and religions and languages and skin tones mixed together like paints. There are two Syrian families, an Eritrean family, a family from South Sudan, a Burundian woman, a few Iraqis, and a family from Congo. One more family from Syria is expected next week. I approach a group of Africans. The men are dressed in button-down shirts and dress pants with flip-flops; the women are a flurry of stiff, colourful cottons.

"Where are you from?" I ask one of the Africans. When you ask a refugee where he is from, he will tell you the last place he lived.

"Toronto."

"No, you're not. Where are you from? Where were you before Toronto?"

"Burundi."

"How many brothers and sisters do you have?"

"I 'ave four brothas. One sista."

I point to a few Africans who have circled us. "Are these your brothers and sisters?"

"No."

"So you're Burundian?"

"No."

"Where were you before Burundi?"

"Congo."

"So Congo, then Burundi, then Toronto, then here?"

"Yes."

This makes sense. He cannot pronounce the letter 'h.' His first language must be French, an official language of Congo. Not an indigenous language, of course, but a protraction of the European scramble for Africa.

"What's your name?"

"Don de Dieu."

"Huh? Don *what*?"

"Don de Dieu. It means Gift of God."

"Oh yes! Dieu! Dieu means God!"

"Yes. Gift of God."

He wears a blue felt cap with a pom-pom on top that looks like something Monet might have worn while painting the French countryside. We are standing in a cluster of tables and chairs.

"Will you help me move these tables and chairs?" I ask him. "I want the chairs in a circle." I don't use tables in the classroom; without the physical barriers of tables, social and emotional barriers come down more quickly.

"Yes." He motions to the Africans, but they are hesitant; they want the tables. Without tables, it's not school; it's not learning. But I want them to experience the substratum of Canadian society: barrier free. Freedom of speech and freedom of movement. Cultures, religions, and values coming together in perfect pitch. This is what we believe.

We move the tables and arrange the chairs into a circle. There is a dented minifridge in the corner and a Cindy Crawford recliner.

"You want?" Shishai, from Eritrea, says.

"No, leave it."

"Yes, yes. For teacher." He moves the recliner into the circle and motions for me to sit.

"Sorry. I can't teach in a recliner." I sit in a chair. He nods his head and takes a seat across from me.

Our class begins with mouth and jaw exercises. We work on vowel sounds, stretching them out like an elastic band, and on pronouncing difficult consonant sounds like 'th' and 'p.' Then we sing. Singing produces proper intonation and stress—it helps students to stress the correct words in a sentence, the correct syllables in a word. Some languages, like Spanish, French, and Cantonese, are syllable-timed: Every syllable is given equal prominence in the sentence, like simple chirps of a sparrow. But English—and Arabic and Russian—are stress-timed: They are unpredictable, like the call of an osprey. Some syllables are clear and long and sharp and press into you, dividing bone and marrow; others are quick and short and crowd into one another like shoppers in Boxing-Day line ups. The students can pronounce the sounds perfectly in song; like birds dipping in pairs, their tongues dip into other worlds. But in conversation, they compress English into their first language, and the two languages will not—*cannot*—come together because they are by nature at odds with one another.

So we sing. And for some students, at some point, things travel from song to speech, change alliances, cross over from death to life. The words become living artefacts within them, taking root and moving through their insides like heaps of fallen leaves swept up by the wind. This is a victory of sorts for the teacher, who seeks to domesticate wild accents—to reduce them and modify them. Not the *people*, of course—but their accents.

Accent reduction is an unpopular term in Canada. We don't say that we want to reduce a person's accent or modify it because the connotation is that we want to modify the *person*—that the *person* is somehow substandard. We don't use such language in Canada. We use political terms that embody notions about liberty and tolerance—and meanwhile, refugees remain unemployed and underemployed because of their accents, because of their poverty, because of their *otherness*: Neurosurgeons scrape the grill at Wendy's, mechanical engineers greet customers at Walmart, and lawyers sort bottles at the depot.

If they *do* carve out a niche in the market, like Vietnamese boat people in the manicure business, we enter into their world, get our feet massaged by a woman who butchers English consonants—but we never invite her to our dinner parties; she is *other*—her speech is *other*—her Mother tongue will not *allow* her to speak proper English because it is free-flowing like a river, and when English deposits boulders in the river, consonants at the ends of words, for example, she simply goes around them. And English-language speakers cannot correct her because social conventions demand that they be polite and innocuous and non-confrontational.

So the two do not speak, and she remains outside social and linguistic conventions. But like a finch without a cage mate, she will die of loneliness if kept by herself. So she gains acceptance, strength, and allegiance from her own subculture, her Mother. And sometimes a subculture will create rules and laws of its own; it will no longer believe itself to be subject to the laws of the land. It becomes a camp, a hidden matrix, subject to its own political space, born into a state of exception—it exists, in essence, outside the normal juridical order. Crimes are no longer crimes. Husbands punish disobedient wives, beat them. Religious leaders teach hatred. And the city recognizes too late that it has created a *campos de concentracion,* that it has an insurrection on its hands.

Every day I go The Booth, and I sing with the refugees until their six months are up and they are carted off to the *campos*: The margins of the city where pawn shops, dollar stores, thrift shops, liquor stores, Vietnamese Pho, pizza parlours, and money changers abound—infirmaries that cater to the perceived needs of the poor but offer little community—nowhere to come together, buy local produce, eat delicious food.

We sing like skylarks, and I think of daybreak; I think of Wordsworth's *To the Skylark* and of *Flanders Fields,* contrasting the beauty of the lark's song with the battle below.

* * *

Our first song is called "Hello, Hello, What's Your Name," sung to the tune of *Mary had a Little Lamb.* I sing the question to individual students, and they sing the answer back to me. I begin with one of the Syrian families, Mohammad and his wife Haya.

"Hello, hello, what's your name, what's your name, what's your name? Hello, hello, what's your name, and how are you today?"

Mohammad sings his response to me: "My name Mohammad, Mohammad Mohammad. My name Mohammad, and I fine todaaaay."

He raises the last note of *today* in a dramatic tenor and holds it for several seconds, extending his arms like Ben Heppner. He is vibrant and playful and he carries the others on the wings of his joy—and his singing fills up the little holes inside of us. I cannot fathom his enthusiasm when I think of what his family has come through. Mohammad was a cab driver in Syria until a bomb went off in his car, ejecting him from the vehicle and blowing his legs off. Now he sits in a rickety wheelchair with a woolen blanket tucked around phantom limbs. I sing the song to his wife Haya, then to the Burundian woman, Esperance. She is too shy to sing the response. She looks down, covers her mouth with her hand.

"Sing," the others say. "We help you. We *help* you!"

They begin to chant, quietly at first, *My name is Esperance, Esperance, Esperance. My name is Esperance, and I am fine today.* Then they raise their voices, louder and louder like percussive cymbals smashing together, and I join in, and we begin to clap and shout in a cacophony of sound that bangs up against the walls and windows: *Esperance, Esperance, my name is Esperance! Esperance, Esperance, my name is Esperance!* We move in close together until there are no pauses between us and every barrier comes down—and then—Esperance says it. She says it: *My name is Esperance.* We clap and cheer and shout and twirl in circles, singing, *Esperance, Esperance, my name is Esperance!* And we've done it. Together, we've done it for Esperance.

Next, we sing about body parts, a song called "Head and Shoulders." This is a tough one. I point to my head, shoulders, knees, and toes as I sing. Some students won't bend over to touch their toes, and I call them on it.

"Touch your toes! Touch your toes!" I won't allow them to sit idle; movement enhances learning. I know this. The second part of the song is difficult, because I want to make word substitutions, teach them other parts of the body. I point to my elbow, then look at Ahmed.

"Ahmed, what's this?"

"Ahmed, what dis," he says.

"No, no. What's this?"

"No, no. What dis! What dis!" He says it exuberantly, as though he has mastered a complex algorithm.

I look at Mayada, point to my elbow.

"Elbow," I say.

"Eh-bow," Ahmed says.

"Yes. Now, Mayada. Elbow."

"Elbow," Mayada says, looking at Ahmed.

Next, I point to my hair and look at Gladys, a student from South Sudan.

"That's your hair," she says. Her English is good. I need her help.

"Gladys, point to something else." I point to different parts of my body to show her what I mean. Gladys points to her eyebrows.

"Eyebrows," she says.

Great, I think. *Eyebrows* has an 'r,' a consonant cluster, and two diphthongs. They'll never get it.

"Okay, we got elbow, hair, and eyebrows. One more." I look at Shishai. "Shishai?"

He touches his cheeks. "Chicks," he says.

"Wonderful! Let's sing." We move through the song several times until they know the tune and the body parts. Each time we sing, I increase the tempo until we are singing so quickly that no one can remember the words, not even me, and we laugh because the teacher doesn't know the words.

"No English," Mohammad says, pointing at me and chuckling.

"No Arabic," I say, pointing back at him.

* * *

This is a good time to tell you about Jedediah. Jedediah is the director of The Booth. He pops his head into my classroom sometimes to watch our antics, and all I can see is a bushy beard and a gold earring—not a face. Occasionally, he joins us when he isn't busy with government or staff or residents or the disasters that seem to occur daily. Most of us call him Jed, but he doesn't like it: He wants to hear the 'ah' in his name. 'Ah' makes him remember his God, Yahweh, and the breath that Yahweh breathed into Adam when he created him, and the breath that he breathed into Abraham and Sarah when he changed their names from Abram and Sarai.

This intrigues me because my name is Sarah. My name has the breath of God in it, Jedediah tells me, like the sound of awe when one encounters a thunderstorm or a waterfall. He says that the people of his homeland, Israel, incorporate the attributes of God into their children's names. In the name Isaiah, for example, or *Yesha'yahu* in the Hebrew, *yesha* means *to save* and *yah* refers to Yahweh, so the name Isaiah proclaims, *Yahweh is salvation*. But the name Yahweh is too holy to utter, so Jed refers to God as HaShem.

Jedediah is an Ashkenazi Jew, from a city called Mary in Turkmenistan, which is bordered by Uzbekistan, Kazakhstan, Afghanistan, Iran, and the Caspian Sea. Persian Jews came from Iran to Turkmenistan in the late 1830's, but most of them fled with the collapse of the Soviet Union. Jed is descended from an original group of about three hundred and fifty individuals who lived in northern France and western Germany, identifying primarily with German customs and the descendants of German Jews. He lived in a refugee home after Turkmenistan split in two, half going to Russia, half to Iran, and that refugee home is a sort of model for The Booth.

"We lived there for one year," he told me, "until a permanent building was constructed for us. We all stayed together, like a flock of birds. We moved together from the refugee home to the permanent apartment building. Families weren't split up like they are here. And everyone in the home had a job to do: cleaning, cooking, childcare."

This is how Jedediah has organized The Booth. Some people look after kids, others cook, others clean. He has a small staff: four counsellors and me. Everything else is done by the refugees.

In Turkmenistan, Jedediah was a physician. He cannot practice in Canada because of his English. His English is exemplary—he understands the movements and tenors of the language better than most native speakers do—but he speaks with an accent. Language learning is a funny thing at advanced levels. It doesn't move forward with your efforts; it pushes against you. The old accent crouches somewhere behind you, but you cannot subsume it without time—lots of time—and meticulous effort.

But you have children to look after or your legs were blown off by a bomb or you are working three jobs—and your mistakes and your accent fossilize, hardening like the rock of a quarry. You begin to feel the shame of it after you've lived in the country for years and years and still can't get out from under its linguistic regime. And government leaders smile for the television cameras and say: *Look what we're doing for refugees! They are welcome here!* They bring them in and call themselves humanitarians. What happens afterwards is inconsequential—at least for now.

Jed has an under-bite like a barracuda, and his face is darkened by deep seams that run around his eyes. He is quiet and watchful. He works at a doctor's office sometimes in the evenings, replaces the paper on the examining beds, washes down equipment, files patient records. At The Booth, he binds people's wounds, diagnoses their illnesses, and listens to their stories through the counsellors, who double as interpreters. This, I think, is his greatest balm: listening to their stories.

* * *

I told you before that I live near a quarry, a reclaimed mine west of Dead Man's Flats in the Bow Valley whose rocks, it turns out, were drenched in cream once—rich and thick and milky, spilling over the sides into a surging new railway. Those rocks had meaning once, and worth: They had a life. But at some point, someone decided that they were no longer profitable, and on Black Friday, 1979, after nearly one hundred years of coal production, the mines were shut down.

They sealed the shafts and the portals, sealed every opening to that former way of life, leaving barely a mark—only an ache in the bones, a feeling that life was galloping toward some small spot on the horizon. And the dogged digging of holes and the fidelity to obscure ideals flickered out with the miners' lamps, and the miners penetrated deeper and deeper into darkness, darker still than any coal mine. They collapsed like semi vertical seams that cave in without warning, because there was nothing beneath them—only midsummer night dreams of blue-black coal. The living continued, though—painfully, in bodies full of dust and dying, but still they wept, thinking of the mines, the only thing they'd known since boyhood.

Starting out at the tipple or the picking table or the boxcars or the briquette plant, waiting for the 7 a.m. whistle—hoping for two whistles instead of one, because two whistles meant there was no work that day—then walking in straight lines to the mines. They walked along the railroad tracks to the washhouse at the tipple; then they changed into their pit clothes and picked up their lamps at the Lamp house. With their coal buckets and their Wolfe safety lamps dangling from their necks, they walked that straight line into the dark places of the earth and tunnelled through the rock, laying bare the roots of the mountains and the rivers, bringing hidden things into the light. Old men and young men—boys, really—drilled, blasted, and loaded broken coal and rock by hand into chutes or mine cars, then pushed the cars out to a horse and driver, who hauled it across the bridge to the CP yard.

If a man worked hard, he could make his way up to pitboss, switcher, conductor, fireman, or even engineer. And so the people came, generations of miners from Ukraine, Wales, England, Ireland, Poland, Italy, Austria, Belgium, Finland, and Slovakia: an archetype of multiculturalism, every branch grafted in until pluralism somehow gave way to monism because it had to; it *had to*. The mining company built a bunkhouse, then a cookhouse, then company houses located close to the mines. Later a hotel and company store were added, then an opera house and a boarding house and a post office. On Saturdays, the men lined up for their pay cheques and went to the Saturday night polkas and listened to the accordion and drank Pilsner beer.

Now, they've taken up the track from the old bridge, planked it so people can walk on it again, and the only roofed mine structure left is the Lamp house. There are caves, too, where the shafts or tunnels have come to the surface after gravel and loose timber bulldozed into the vertical slots settled and collapsed into a sinkhole. The surface appears solid, but it's unstable, and sometimes the sinkholes erupt.

The quarry—an open-pit mine—was filled in with water and stocked with Arctic grayling. A solitary loon lives there now. His eyes are red and his bones are solid, not hollowed-out like the bones of most birds. He dives deep, and sometimes he stays underwater for up to five minutes. If you look deep like the loon, you can see the miners' black faces and the Wolfe lanterns around their necks.

Everything is under the surface now; everything is invisible—like the refugees, their former lives scraped clean and sealed off, bits and pieces and small moments gliding past dreamlike—but with anguish, butting up against a perplexing world of cold, and dark mornings.

I live alone at the quarry, like the loon. My father never liked it.

"A young woman ought not to live alone," he used to tell me. "You ought to live with your family. Until you are married."

I know this. I can't explain why I need the quarry. I am an only child. Maybe that's it. I grew up in solitude. I grew up in the Bow Valley, climbing the Rocky Mountains. I learned the stories of the peaks: Ha Ling, Miner's Peak, Mount Rundle, Lady MacDonald, the Three Sisters. When my parents moved to the city, I couldn't leave. I couldn't leave the quarry, that diamond-shaped pane of glass bevelled at the edges, hemming me in behind and before, holding the images of the peaks and conveying utterances from one discursive world to another—from Heaven to Earth—in a dialectic whose sole objective is movement, back and forth. I was in my twenties when my parents left—old enough to live alone. But I should be married by now. I know that.

* * *

It's April. Not much snow is left on Ha Ling, except in the creases of its skin, small pockets of white tucked in like tissue into an old woman's brassiere. I hike Ha Ling in the mornings, before English class. It takes an hour to summit. I like the climbing; I like the struggle in it, the solitude, the rocks and ridges and the unambiguous sky. At the summit, there's a cache buried under some loose rock. Inside the cache is an American dime, an Aberhart Trojans medal, a key chain, a sticky label for a jam jar, a few business cards, and a 1988 Olympic Games pin. The idea is to take something out and leave something behind. I take the pin, leave nothing behind.

There are some papers and a pencil in the cache so you can write a poem or a message. I read the notes. Stupid stuff, mostly: "Jimmy was here and sober"; "Beautiful view"; "Made it up alive." There's also a drawing of an alien. Beneath the alien is a poem about Turkey, about the little Kurdish refugee who drowned in the Mediterranean Sea and woke up the collective conscience—woke it up and hauled it out of bed:

> boy face down
> water nudging
> boy won't stir
> fathers wailing
> wet sand heavy
> mawsim coming
> thick like war

The wind picks up a swirl of red-breasted finches and flings them deep into a canyon between the peaks, reminding them of some great omnipotence beyond them. Everything is tiny on the mountaintop—chipmunks, spiders, wildflowers, berries—tiny and insignificant, as if competing with the mountain is futile, as if it's futile to even try. But Ha Ling tried, in 1896. That's the story of this mountain. Ha Ling was Chinese, a town cook for the miners. One day, the other cooks bet him fifty dollars that he couldn't climb the peak, plant a flag on the summit, and make it back in less than ten hours. It couldn't be done, they said. Ha Ling started his ascent at 7 a.m. and was back in time for lunch. And the mountain was named after him.

First they called it Chinaman's Peak, because as a Chinese, his name—his humanity—wasn't as important as his Chinese orientation, as someone who was *other*. That name, Chinaman's, fell out of vogue at some point when social conventions determined that Ha Ling did in fact have a level of humanity. And they named a mountain after him. And if you examine the tiny blue wildflowers along the path, and you see their complexity, you realize that small things can indeed compete with a mountain.

* * *

I run down Ha Ling—it's steep—and drive to The Booth listening to Andrea Bocelli—*Ava Maria, The Prayer, When I Fall in Love*. Inside the front door of The Booth, there's a foyer with a few chairs and a stained carpet. It needs to be taken up. To the left is a reception area and a sign-in sheet. The main floor is shaped like an Arabic "n": a "u" with a dot over it. The dot is the kitchen and dining area. The 'u,' a horseshoe, is a hallway that holds the guest rooms. It is swaddled in computer-generated photos of former students—dozens and dozens of them tacked to the walls, filling the 'u' with images of transience like crocuses in old snow.

Each room has a lock on the door—a little bolt on the inside—but Jedediah's room, just off the bottom of the 'u,' the place where you grip a horseshoe to throw it—is the only room without a lock. Everyone eats and rests and socializes in the central dining room. That is the focal point of the home: Just as the dot makes the *nun*, so the kitchen makes The Booth. My classroom is in the basement, under Jed's office.

In the classroom, the students are seated, waiting for me, because I'm late. It doesn't matter, they tell me; time is stretchy in their cultures. The Syrians are there, the Iraqis and the Burundian woman, and the Eritreans, South Sudanese, and Congolese. But the new family still has not arrived. Chickadees are on the windowsill. We gather together, form a circle. I begin by singing the greeting song to Hamid, from Iraq. Hamid is blind in one eye, it looks like; I can never tell which way he is looking. He smiles because he recognizes the song—he's starting to learn English. His teeth are bad, loosely hinged and dark at the gums. He sings his response to me, then turns to his wife, Fedva.

"Hello, hello, what you name, what you name, what you name? Hello, hello, what you name, and how you today?"

The students laugh because Hamid is asking his wife what her name is. Hamid was an engineer in Iraq—before the police came to his home to kill him. He designed cars. Now he has oppressive fatigue and bullet holes in his arms and legs and in his soul. But he wants to give back; he wants to work. He wants his family to succeed. He wants to find a house in the centre of the city, away from the edges, because in the centre the schools are better. He knows this, somehow, within a few days of arriving.

I sing the song to Esperance. She smiles, covers her mouth with her hand, and looks down. Is it the words or the melody that she can't articulate? I'm not certain. Gladys says something to her in Swahili and begins to hum the tune to *Mary had a Little Lamb*. Esperance joins in. I'm grateful. It's enough, I think, if she learns the melody. The words will come later. And I wonder if my singing and my words—if all of my efforts—are in vain. Because I can't think of another human being who has endured the things that Esperance has—her family killed, she and her sister taken hostage and gang raped.

Later, after finding work as a housekeeper, her employer raped her, and her first child was conceived. She has three other children. I don't know where they came from. How does she cope with even the simple stresses of her existence? What fixations of mind propel her through the days? I wonder if her past has obliterated every propensity for independent thought and initiative. Because I see in her and in others the fear of living away from the fence line—like Holocaust survivors who, after liberation, could not bear the soft touch of a mattress and slept on wooden floors.

"Esperance, let's try something else. Head and Shoulders." I point to my head. "What's this?"

She puts her hands on her head, looks at me, says nothing. She reminds me of a small child, but she's not a child: She's a grown woman with four children. There are little bite marks on her arms. Bed bugs, maybe. I shift my chair a little, move away from her.

"Head," I say.

"H, h, h."

"Good. Now, head. Head. Head."

"Head." Her eyes are fastened on mine, sharp and attentive.

"Shoulders."

"Shoo-ers."

"Shoul-DERS." I shout out the "d" to accentuate it.

Esperance shouts as well. "Shoo-DERS."

The rest of the class is getting restless. I'm losing them.

Don de Dieu's English is good. I solicit his help. "Don de Dieu, would you lead us through the song?"

Don de Dieu moves through the song and the motions, and the class follows him, pronouncing head as -ead, without the 'h,' like he does. Oh well. We sing a few more songs and then have a snack—a time to practice skills in conversation. Jedediah brings the food: carrots, celery, humus, pita, and juice. The students cut vegetables, break up pita, put the humus in a bowl, pour the juice. The task of preparing food facilitates language, gives it a place to breathe. Everyone helps except Ahmed. He sits, arms folded, and watches. Jed brings him a plate of food, sits with him.

* * *

"What the hell is wrong with that guy?" I ask Jed later in his office during coffee break. He's seated behind his desk, arms folded across his chest, legs stretched out; I can see his bare feet under the desk. I don't know where his shoes and socks are. The office is lime green with black furniture and a Persian carpet. The black fuses with the green, lowers its pitch like the green you see on copper basins or at the base of a flame. There's an ant farm sitting in a large tub of water next to the door.

"Why is your ant farm in a sink of water?

"It's a moat. Prevents them from escaping. I had petroleum jelly before—on the sides of the formicary—but they built bridges over it."

There's a large book case with several tattered books, the spines coming off one or two and pages coming out of the others. No cover on another. They aren't lined up like they should be; they are stacked in incongruous piles, some of them on the floor: Einstein, Newton, Ramanujan, Galileo, Ada Yonah. Shakespeare and Bialik.

Mostly, the office looks like a high-school science experiment. There's a poster of the periodic table tacked to the wall and a long table behind Jed's desk with beakers and lighters and small stuffed rodents and butterflies and beetles pinned to thin slabs of wood. There's a sink in the corner filled with beakers, stained coffee cups, forks and knives and little Chinese plates, and beside the sink is a table with a microscope on it. I bend over and take a look. Turn a few dials.

"Don't touch that," Jed says to me.

I straighten up and look around. "This place is a mess."

"It's not. I know where everything is. Everything."

"Okay ... where's the book by Albert Einstein?"

"Bookcase. Where it should be. Look. About Ahmed ... "

"Wrong—it's not in the bookcase. It's on the floor."

"That's what I said. Look. Don't think of Ahmed's value system as ... as a parody, simply because it is incongruous with the images you inherited from your ancestors."

"That's the point. My ancestors were democratic. You know, equal rights?"

"But democracy *confines* you; it confines you to the wilderness of your own soul. You cast your vote, and your whole destiny is in your own hands."

"That's the point."

"But you stand alone in a democracy. Democracy turns you in on yourself. It inverts you."

"So you prefer to be subsumed by a dictator?"

"No. I prefer to be governed by HaShem. And by those he places over me. I think ... in some ways, I think Ahmed's worldview is superior to yours, Sarah. He at least acknowledges that there is a power greater than himself—a power to whom he is accountable."

"So that's why everyone is banging on our Canadian doors? Scrambling to get underneath our—our democratic wing?"

"Well ... I think democracy ... How do I say this. I think democracy— and certainly capitalism—is *itself* a dictator of sorts. Because it constantly mediates our thoughts and our behaviour and our prejudices. But we have to *test* our prejudices. We have to have a wider breadth of vision so we can—so we can look beyond what is close at hand. So we can see better—see our prejudices within a larger whole."

"How can anyone see beyond their own circumstances?"

He sits upright, raking his beard with his fingers, pulling it into a small point at the bottom and twisting it into a thin stream of hair.

"Well. Sarah. Every *system*, I think—every unity of meaning ... is, is resonant in the collective unconscious. It just *is*. Think of our judicial system. A court decision is never arbitrary; the entire body of law bears down upon it. Ahmed, too, is a law unto himself—but he is part of a larger body, a larger history that flows through him. And that's—that's really beautiful."

"But he's in Canada now. He needs to figure it out."

He looks at me, doesn't answer. I try to soften the edges of my remark.

"He needs to learn Canadian values. So he can survive here. And I don't know where that line is, you know? How do I teach our values and at the same time encourage him to retain his own? And what do I do when, when *his* values undermine *my* way of life? I mean, let's face it. We're talking about freedom. I mean, I see the way things are going. I've read about the first stages of Jihad. Move in. Keep the peace, follow the laws. Have lots of children—lots. I don't think I'd look good in a hijab, you know?"

He glances at the lime, windowless walls housing the periodic table, and his earring takes on the green, looking more like copper than gold.

"Do you remember who you are, Sarah?"

"What?"

"Do you remember who you are?"

"What are you talking about?"

"You are a teacher."

"I know that."

"A teacher is like a rabbi. In Hebrew—and in the Arabic cognate—the root for rabbi means master. Or great one. Someone worthy of respect."

"That resonates."

He doesn't crack a smile. He's immune to humour.

"Perhaps you should start playing the part."

I'm incensed. "I'm excellent at what I do."

"Yes." He pauses for several moments. I wait. Am I supposed to stand here until hell freezes over while he collects his thoughts? I move toward the door.

"Have you ever eaten with them?" he asks. "Have you ever *eaten* with them?"

"Of course I have," I say over my shoulder. "We have snacks every bloody day. Veggies and humus. Twinkies, even."

"Have you ever stayed after class. Joined them for a meal in the dining room? Have you ever moved beyond educating them?"

I stop. Turn toward him. "You want me to work *overtime*?"

He moves his hands through his hair, pulls it back. His face has tones of grey. "Sar-ah," he says, sighing, holding the ah for just a moment. "Man looks at the outward appearance. HaShem looks at the heart. Try to look beyond your own horizon." He takes out a notepad and begins scribbling notes in sprawling, circular script. "We need to make some changes. The new family is coming. Their room needs work."

The ants are tunnelling deep into caverns; big, black, repulsive things.

"Why don't you throw in some red ones? Mix things up a bit?"

"You mean like army ants? No. I can't do that. Army ants are abominable. They loot food from their enemies, kill those in their own ranks, even. They even ... well, they even engage in cannibalism—and they conduct what we would call—something akin to suicide bombings. You can't mix certain breeds."

"Ants and humans are a lot alike."

"There are similarities, I guess. Especially when it comes to warfare. Large-scale, tactical warfare. The size of the army and the strategic placement of troops—well, all of that is more important than the *calibre* of troops. Red ants accumulate *hordes* of troops, somehow, and then they move forward in a massive, united front to overwhelm the enemy."

"Sounds like WWII."

"Yes—but different, too. There's not really a central command or a hierarchy in ant armies. They're more like networks. They're like, well—they're kind of like terrorist networks."

He sighs, then sinks into his work, like he's forgotten that I'm there. A few children rush into the room. Jed's office is the place where children gather. They come to do experiments: They make volcanoes with vinegar and baking soda, play music with aluminum rods, mix liquids with piquant odours, find the centre of gravity for books and pencils and coffee cups. I have no idea how Jed gets any work done.

I return to my classroom, annoyed. He asks too much of me. I gather the students into a circle and begin singing *Boom Chicka Boom*, an echo song similar to a canon. For this song, the leader shouts out *Boom Chicka Boom* and performs an accompanying action, and the others imitate him. I ask Mayada to take the lead. She's uncertain at first, then raises one arm and sweeps it back and forth like a pendulum butting up against invisible barriers.

"Boo chick boo."

The other students, both men and women, follow her lead. She raises her other arm and begins to turn her hands in the rhythms of the song, never transgressing the limits of her pendular field. And I wonder if these limits are a sort of metaphor—whether they confine her or offer greater definition, greater depth of being. Ahmed remains still, doesn't raise his arms, and I ask him to lead.

"Teacher," he says, pointing at me. "Teacher sing."

His paradigms will not yield—not today. I nod my head and sing, mounting an invisible horse and riding it. The students follow me, swinging lassoes above their heads. We're chanting *Boom Chicka Boom*, riding our horses like cowboys, and Jed walks in.

He sits down, asks the students to join him.

"Students—Sarah—I have an announcement."

There's a light tap on the door. It's a little African boy in a grey sweat suit.

"Sarah, this is my son, Amos," Gladys says. "Can he sit in with us today?"

"No kids. Sorry."

"He's sick."

"Well … okay. Only if he's quiet."

The last thing I need is a little kid disrupting my class. Amos takes off his shoes and places them neatly at the door. He steps gingerly, head down, eyeing each adult from beneath his tapered brows. He sits on the floor at Gladys' feet and folds his hands in his lap.

"Does he need some crayons or something?"

"He's fine."

Jed is watching Sadya, a rakish woman, her hair overrun with a riot of curls. She's complacent today, and he notices immediately.

"Sadya? What's wrong?"

She folds her hands, looks down.

"Sadya, what's happened?"

"They came yesterday," she responds, her voice cracking. "To my village in Iraq. Lined up one hundred youth. Shot them. Push bodies in river." Her voice is rising. She looks directly at Mohammad. He is Muslim. She is Christian.

"*Why*?" she shouts at him. "Why this evil? *Why*?" Her voice booms around the room like a gong. No one moves. I can feel my tongue sticking to the roof of my mouth.

Mohammad is gentle and non-combative. "Sorry. I sorry," he says. "I so sorry." His words fall softly, and she is placated, speaks in quieter tones.

"All these people. I knew them. I am *here* now. Why? *Why*?" She begins to sob. There is nothing we can say, nothing we can give. Mohammad wheels over to her, places his hand on her shoulder. She stops sobbing, startled. A man touching a woman. A married man touching another woman.

"I very, very sorry." His voice is pleading, like the high notes of a violin.

Jedidiah watches Mohammad, his mouth slightly open, his bottom row of teeth jutting out. And a tender shoot unfurls: a shoot of love between a Jew and an Arab, germinated in the soil of Sadya's heartbreak.

"Sadya," Jed says, "are you okay?"

Gladys begins to rummage through her purse. She fishes out a stockpile of pens and pencils, crumpled papers, chipped Tylenols, two cell phones, and three Hot Wheels before finding a packet of Christie crackers.

"Here. Have these."

She taps Amos on the shoulder and he brings Sadya the crackers, his lips pursed into a little "o," then returns to Gladys's feet. Sadya opens the crackers and rubs one between her fingertips. The holes get larger as the substance around them breaks off, and small perforated pieces fall into her lap.

"I'm okay," she says to Jed. "Say your announcement."

Jedediah hesitates for several moments.

"One of our new families is coming next week. From Syria," he says. He looks at Sadya. She's quiet, looking down. How crass, I think, that he would carry on like nothing has happened. It's not until later, much later, that I gain a thin coat of understanding: When you attend to incidentals at the surface, the reality—the *immensity* of it all—moves underground.

"We are going to make some changes to their rooms. We will begin by painting the walls. The room needs colour." He waits while the advanced students, Gladys and Don de Dieu and Sadya, translate for those who don't understand. "We need to repair the furniture and decorate. Make it ready for them. We will begin tomorrow afternoon. No English class." He looks at me.

"Sar-ah, you can come and help or take the day off."

He reminds me of a raven. Ravens make other animals do their tasks for them. Their beaks cannot open the tough skins of carcasses, so they make vocalizations that attract wolves and foxes to a kill site, and the large carnivores open the carcass, exposing the meat.

* * *

The Sparrowhawk tarns are south of Ha Ling. It's not too difficult to reach them: After a few steep pitches and some minor bouldering, you come into a wide, open space—a large cirque that was excavated by a glacier—and there are small tarns all around. At the beginning of the season, the tarns are deep and green, but by late July they shallow out into muddy brown rings like day-old coffee settled into the bottom of a cup. At the highest tarn, someone has built a monument to King Arthur and his knights: a flat, roundish table with four tall chairs around it, all created from large stones found in the cirque.

I'm seated at the table, trying to decide what to do. Do I go to The Booth, make a good impression? Or spend the morning exploring the tarns? The ground around me is soft and marshy. I take off my boots and socks and wade into a small tarn, its soft, creamy mud clinging to the hollows of my feet. I am completely alone. There are no grizzlies up here in the spring; they are at lower elevations eating roots and rodents. Some of the hiking trails have been roped off into no-go zones because a bumper crop of berries is expected this year, and the bears will soon be threatening people, guarding their religion like patriots without a nation.

Grizzlies are like guerrillas—ubiquitous and sublime all at once, operating on ambiguous terrain, inciting fear through unpredictability: An attack can come from anywhere, anytime, by any means, by any member of the population. This forces the people and the wardens into a state of hyper-arousal. Wardens police the bears with a traditionalist sort of biopower; they track their movements, put collars on them, and live with them in a cold war, adopting counterinsurgency strategies to control them—but control is always provisional, always limited, always resisted.

I rinse my feet, wipe off the water with my socks. Put on the wet socks and my boots. I'll go to The Booth, I decide. I don't really have a choice. After a ninety-minute descent, I'm near the bottom of the trail walking through patches of pine and spruce and aspen. There's a thin haze veiling the mountains today; they look like dry bones rising up out of the earth— no skin or flesh. I stop and listen periodically, look for bear scat. I don't wear bear bells, don't carry bear spray, don't make noise. I should. I know that. Counterinsurgency. The path narrows through the woods. I can't see more than a few meters in front of me, and the Earth's iron has spread over everything a reddish-orange rind. Silent wilderness is all around.

I stop and listen. I smell something wet, something dank. There's a bear in the area, I think. Close by. Visions of teeth and jaws and claws break into my mind, and I begin to run. I shouldn't: If a bear is ahead of me, running will startle it, bring me upon it more quickly. But terror usurps reason, and I rush along the pathway, bend after bend, branches scraping my face and arms and drawing blood. I stumble over roots and rocks until finally—finally—the road is in view. I slow down, look behind me. Nothing. Nothing is there. Only a hollow sky, a great, excavated cirque, and a head full of fantasies, illogical fear, and phobia: *Ursus arctos horribilis*, family *Ursidae*.

I can't go to The Booth empty handed; I should bring something for the new family. I pick up a gift on the way: delicate salt and pepper shakers made of crystal. When I arrive, a few of the men are painting the family's room: Mohammad, Ahmed, and Don De Dieu.

"Red and yellow and pink and green," Mohammad exclaims when he sees me, repeating the lyrics of a song that I've taught them, *I Can Sing a Rainbow*. They are using burnt-orange paint, lining the edges of the walls with small brushes.

"Where's Jed?" I ask.

"Store."

"Oh. Okay. I'll start rolling." I get some paint and a roller and begin to apply the paint in large swaths, which I prefer to the refined, finicky work that the men are doing. Children are running in and out, and I swat at them when they get too close to me. We work until the shadows turn bloody orange, and then Jedediah arrives with two of the ladies. Their arms are laden with shopping bags, and Jed is carrying a long carpet. As soon as he comes into the room, the children swarm around him.

"Fire!" they shout. "Make fire!"

Jed grins, a bit sheepishly. "I don't know what they're talking about," he says. "It's their English, I think. I think it's their poor English."

"Come and see what we got," Gladys says. Esperance is beside her, smiling, covering her mouth with her hand.

We gather around as Gladys unpacks the supplies: a teapot and cups, a small table, a mirror, a poster of Einstein, blankets and sheets. Big pillows to sit on.

"I have something," I say. I fetch the salt and pepper shakers from my purse, set them beside the other supplies.

"They won't use those," Gladys says.

"Oh."

"Let's take a break," Jed says. "We'll set everything up later. Sar-ah, will you eat with us? Everything is ready. The ladies have been cooking."

I feel awkward. It's one thing to work with people; it's quite another to socialize with them. I don't like to socialize. I like to be alone.

"Come on, baby doll," Gladys says, taking my hand and leading me into the dining room. The dining room and kitchen used to flow together through an opening in the wall, but Jed boarded it up. He wanted to shut off the kitchen; he wanted the kitchen, and all that went on in it—the cutting of animals and grinding them, putting them through the fire—to remain outside the camp, as it were—outside the place where people gather. Like the back country, where you hang food and deodorant and soap and anything with a scent high in the trees, outside the camp, so predators are not drawn in.

There's a battered piano in the corner of the dining room and several round tables with chairs. Mohammad is sitting in his wheelchair next to one of the tables.

"Please. Sit," he says to me. He is the host tonight, I think. We all sit. I'm at a table with Ahmed, Mayada, and their four children. The Africans and Arabs are mixed around the other tables, buzzing with movement and activity; children are up and down, between legs, on shoulders, in arms. Haya and Fedva bring bowls of pita and chicken and rice and sauces and set them on the tables.

"What about you?" I ask Mohammad.

"I ate before," he says.

I know this isn't true. I know he wants to preside over my meal because I am an honoured guest, because I have never eaten with the students before.

There is no cutlery. I take a piece of pita, put a little rice and chicken in it and nibble at the edges. Mohammad and his family are watching. Ahmed and *his* family are watching.

"How do I do this?" I ask. "Like this?"

"No, no, no!" Mohammad wheels up to the table. He grasps some chicken and rice between his thumb and forefingers, squeezes the food into a ball, dips it in a sauce, then flicks it into his mouth with his thumb. He opens his mouth wide and laughs, and bits of rice fall on his lips. Ahmed too dives into the bowl, then his wife and children also eat. Haya and Fedva bring more meats and sauces and salads, then mints and baklava—and then coffee. Haya brings a tray of tiny cups and a thermos— and right then, I think of my father. My father, who always told me that I was the cream in his coffee.

"Me," Ahmed says, tapping his chest. "Me."

He stands, takes the thermos from Haya and pours the dark liquid into a cup, then places the cup before me. He nods at me.

"Good," he says, "good."

I look at the coffee, but I'm so moved by the gesture that I cannot drink. I know the boundaries that Ahmed has crossed to serve a woman. Jedediah is sitting at an adjacent table, and he is watching me, his face dark and fierce with emotion.

I take a sip. It tastes like tinged black licorice. "What is the spice in this?" I ask Ahmed.

He calls to Haya in Arabic, and she comes to the table.

"What is the spice?" I ask her, holding up my cup.

"Arabic spice ... ummm, how you say?"

"Licorice? Black licorice?"

"Yes. Spice."

"Thank you," I say to Ahmed. He pats his chest and sits down.

"Syrians best cooks in Middle East," Haya says. She looks at Mohammad.

"Best," he says. "Every country in Middle East knows this."

He pulls up his wheelchair, and Haya sits down.

"Haya is delicious," he says.

"How many letters are there in Arabic?" I ask, embarrassed by his remark.

"Twenty-eight," Mohammad says.

"Do you have vowels and consonants, like English?"

"Paper. I get paper." He wheels back from the table, but Jedediah interjects.

"No, Mohammad. Don't worry. I have paper in the office." He disappears for a few moments, returns with a pad of paper and a pen, sits down with us.

"Look," Mohammad says. Taking the paper and pen, he draws a series of hooks and dots and loops, right to left, beautiful like the curves of a violin.

"How do you write, *good cook*?" I ask. He writes it, and I hold up the paper to Haya. She smiles and clasps her hands together.

"How do you write, *good student*?"

Again Mohammad writes the message, and I give the paper to Ahmed. He nods and pats his chest.

"Now I have a message for *you*, Mohammad. How do you write, *bad student*?" I ask, winking at Haya.

"No, no. I write message for *you*." He moves his wrist in elaborate circles and produces my message.

"What does it say? What does it *say*?"

"Cannot tell you," he says, chuckling, cocking his head.

"Tell me! What does it *say*?"

"It say, *bad teacher!*"

I snatch the paper from him, crumple it up and throw it on the floor. He laughs. "Okay. Message for Jed." He looks at Jedediah, his face serious now, like a winter sky, overcast and bright all at once. He writes the message, hands it to Jed. Jed bows slightly, folds the paper, puts it in his breast pocket.

"Aren't you going to look at it?" I ask.

"I will read it later," Jed says. He strokes his beard and studies me for a moment. "Thank you for coming. The students—the students were honoured."

Blood rushes to my face: I'm blushing. I hate that—being so transparent. "It wasn't so bad," I say. "But I should go."

"Don De Dieu is going to play the piano for us. Why don't you stay?"

"I really can't."

"Why are you afraid?" He's looking at me with those black eyes, deep like the tarns, his beard all around.

I am torn. I want to stay, but Jed is right: I'm afraid. When I'm teaching, I'm in control. But here? Eating and talking on a level plain? It's too much. And there's something else. I'm afraid of *them*. I'm afraid of what they want from us. What they will take from us. I move my chair closer to Jed and lower my voice.

"I'm afraid that their war will become our war," I finally say.

"It already is. It always has been. The earth belongs to HaShem, Sarah, not to us. He owns the cattle on a thousand hills. He tells the stars when to come out at night. He determines the exact times and places people will live. You cannot kick against the goads, Sar-ah."

"It's just this. We're bringing in all these refugees. But we don't have the resources to look after them, so they end up on welfare. We're becoming a welfare state."

"Okay, well. What's the answer? Where should they go? Do you prefer a world of apartheid?"

"I think we're beyond that ... but I think we need to share the load. You know, global community and all that?"

"Do you know how many refugees are flooding into Uganda, Congo, and Kenya from South Sudan alone? The Earth belongs to HaShem. Why do you think you have special rights just because you were born *here*?"

"Because we follow the rules. Because we work hard. And now we should just throw it away? We have a moral obligation to do our part—I know that. But we shouldn't compromise our own security, our children's future, in the process." A sour taste comes into my mouth as I say the words.

"Yesterday on my way to work, I saw a small pothole in the road. It was chalked off, ready to be repaired. Could we not live with that pothole and instead help one refugee?"

"But then *our* way of life is compromised. Everything we've worked for—everything that draws people here."

I can't help but be agitated; not because he is pressing me, but because I recognize competing truths within myself. I want some kind of unifying theory like Einstein did—a governing principle that subsumes all else, brings all things into one accord, makes all things reasonable. But like Einstein, I cannot find it. I think of my Mennonite background. My father. Things I've always believed because I'm supposed to, because I always have. Because the foundations can't come down. I watch the students. They've finished eating, and they are moving the tables and chairs into a large horseshoe, a *nun*, with the piano as the dot.

"I'm a patriot, I guess. I don't want to see my country destroyed because its social systems are weighed down."

He thinks for a moment. "You know, I was just reading about that the other day."

"Reading about what?"

"Patriotism." He furrows his brow.

"Uh huh ... "

"Well, this book said—well, I think it was a book—I can't remember. Maybe it was a journal article."

"For God's sake, what did it say?"

"Well, it said that in the Middle Ages and the Renaissance, the love of country wasn't really tied to a country's institutions, or ... or to its national identity. The idea of loving one's country—well, it wasn't about nationalism as *we* understand it. It was about ... *amor* ... *amor humanitatis*—do you know that term? *Amor humanitatis*? It's a love of *humanity*; it's a love of *all* nations. Nationalism is a distortion of that idea—of that, of that *tradition*; nationalism—patriotism—as we know it, was consummated in the fascist regimes of the twentieth century."

He's silent again. I wait. He smoothes out his moustache with his thumb and forefinger. His fingers are thick and pulpy. Dirt under the nails.

"The only possible response to the refugee crisis, Sar-ah," he finally says, "is *amor humanitatis*."

That is so damn naïve, I think. What does he think? Does he think he can create another European Union here at The Booth? Stitch things back together and hope they'll hold? Replace religion and race with some kind of para-national amalgamation?

"You can't bury those wounds," I say. "Someone, sometime, will let them out of the box again."

Even as I say the words, I am aware that perhaps *I* am the one who is naïve, adopting dusty, fascist notions about war and state. Lop off the head and you'll kill the beast. Jed's wisdom and intellect are encyclopaedic, but I wonder how his theory of *amor humanitatis* would hold up if he knew that I was German, that my grandfather was a member of the Nazi Party. Would he, as a Jew, still be willing to create a mantle of forgetfulness and forgiving?

I think of my father, of his guilt and shame over the Holocaust. *We are evil people*, I heard him say once. I remember this. He was folded up into a kitchen chair at the aluminum table, hair thinned out like a dandelion gone to seed. Hands cupped around a coffee mug, taking sips between the chips on the rim. I, seated beside him, erect, not knowing what to do with his emotion.

"Or would you prefer to remain in your Platonic cave," Jed is saying to me.

I snap back to the present. "What?"

"Do you prefer your Platonic cave. In the mountains."

"Well … it's more of a shire, I think."

"Ah, yes. Hobbits. They live underground, don't they?"

"Well, yes. But they're not real, you know."

He looks at my feet, fitted with size-ten Birkenstocks. "I'm not so sure."

I emit a snicker and then quickly pull it back again. His face is deadpan. He's calling me a hobbit. A halfling.

"You prefer the shadows," he says.

"There are no shadows without light, Jed."

He laughs a little, perhaps because the halfling has matched wits with a wizard. He looks at the students, yearning on his face. Don De Dieu starts on the piano: Strauss waltzes. He is wearing his blue felt cap, and the pompom is dangling by a string, rolling in the music. The students move around the piano, hemming it in; some are dancing, some are chatting, some are singing, layering their Mother tongues on top of the melodies. The African cottons look like multi-coloured pinwheels against the battered beige walls, and the Muslim women in their black gowns look like actors in shadow theatre. Everything comes alive, somehow, around that battered vertical piano.

"Don De Dieu," Jedediah shouts. "Where did you learn Strauss?"

"Germany." He keeps banging on the keys, and the music and the students are spinning and lengthening into a sorbet of loose limbs and clapping hands and stamping feet.

"How did you end up in Germany?" I shout.

"Excuse me? I don't understand."

"Why did you go to Germany?"

He stops playing, comes over and sits with us. "My people. They are animals. Behaving like animals." He shakes his head mournfully. "I escaped. Germany. Learned to play in refugee camp. Small keyboard." And I wonder how many opportunities, how many dreams he has lost. He himself probably doesn't—couldn't possibly know. Does he contemplate the joys that could have been his?

The dancing and singing slowly unwind and come to a stop. Don De Dieu takes off his cap, places it in his lap. The pompom is dangling to the side. He twists it one way, then the other.

"Your pompom is coming off," I say. "Let me sew it for you."

"No, no. Not necessary."

"Jed, do you have a needle and thread?"

"Yes. In the office. You see? My office has everything you need." He smiles briefly, goes to his office, returns with a needle and a spool of red thread. "Is red okay?" he asks Don De Dieu.

"Yes. It's okay." He passes me the cap like it's a communion tray. I thread the needle and sew a few stitches, then pass the cap back to him. He regards it closely, wrapped at the base in crimson, the blue ball sprouting out like a tassel on the hem of a rabbi's robe, then he places it on his head carefully, tilts it slightly to the right. He doesn't thank me.

There is a small, battered case on the floor beside the piano. Mohammad wheels over to it.

"Trumpet. Should not be on floor," he says. "Like holy book." He picks it up gingerly, removes the trumpet from its purple lining in the case, and brings it to Jedediah.

"Jedediah," he says, "you play. Play trumpet."

And it seems to me that Mohammad is holding competing truths, one in each hand: Jed in one hand and the Quran in the other. It seems to me that they are incongruous.

Jedediah presses his lips into the mouthpiece and begins to play *Time to Say Goodbye* in a long, agonizing cry, like the call of an osprey, ancient of days. I know the song. Translated into many languages, it takes on different hues with each language it embodies. But Jed's trumpet says all that needs to be said.

He stops playing suddenly. "Do you know the lyrics, Sarah?"

"Yes. Andrea Bocelli sings it."

"Will you sing with me?"

"Sing with a trumpet? I can't."

"You can," he says. And he begins to sing:

> Time to say goodbye
> to countries I never
> saw and shared with you,
> now, yes, I shall experience them.
> I'll go with you
> on ships across seas
> which, I know,
> no, no, exist no longer.
> It's time to say goodbye.

His singing is like the scent of cloves breathed in deep.

"What is it meaning?" Mohammad asks.

"It is about two people who love each other," Jed says. "Saying goodbye to their old ways. Hoping for a new life together." He looks at Mohammad, then at me.

I'm heating up again. I stand and bow slightly to the students. "Thank you. Thank you for the wonderful meal and the company." They don't understand all the words, but they understand the intent.

"See you soon," a few of them sing, repeating a song I've taught them. So many cultures and customs in this house, under this roof, coexisting like the Eden we've always dreamed about—Eden in all its wonder, all its beauty and its hiddenness, standing just beyond the barbed-wire fence and the trees and the silence of the land, unfurling only briefly in soft murmurs, because you cannot remake history; you cannot make it begin again.

Haya approaches me, brushes my cheeks two times with a kiss.

"Good bye," she says.

"Good bye!" I feel myself coming undone like Don de Dieu's pompom. I turn away and rush out of the dining room and past the kitchen—its stainless steel winking at me, its dishes piled up, grunge pressed into the seams of the linoleum floor. I walk outside and breathe. Jump into my old Jeep, drive the straight road that leads to a pond at the base of the mountains, where every spring, trumpeter swans come for a two-week sojourn in their migration. I pass Yamnuska and the Three Sisters and pull up to my home—but I don't go inside. I walk through the woods to the open grasses around the quarry—the looking-glass with bevelled edges where I know—I *know*—I will find clarity.

I stand, quiet, and watch the quarry, listen to its stories. They called this place a melting pot when the coal was being mined. Ukraine, Wales, England, Ireland, Poland, Italy, Austria, Belgium, Finland, and Slovakia all came to God's country. Put differences aside—hung them high in the trees—and made a life for themselves. They found an Eden of sorts—at least that's how they remember it. But in reality, the cultural topography mirrored the complex geology of the mines, with coal seams that folded and faulted and sometimes disappeared altogether, and—laden with methane gas—were prone to sudden outbursts of coal and gas, overcoming the miners. Sometimes the roof caved in and the coal started to flow and expand and fill the work area, crushing the miners—until finally, the company sawmill erected timber supports to brace the roof rock—but that didn't bring back the men who died, died with Elysian ideals loaded on their backs.

I look back at the woods, and three wolves are standing in the trees, watching me. They're not coyotes. I know the difference. I've seen coyotes in the open field, heads down, pouncing on small prey with legs like springs, caught up in a wind of play and laughter. But wolves live in the woodlands: Their legs are long like the trees. The three wolves stand on the border of the woods, still like the air, and they watch me. They do not move. The land is vacant except for the water and the peaks and the trees. There is nothing else. The wolves stand still and watch me and they do not move.

I'm not afraid, exactly. I'm caught up in the magnetic energy rushing out from them and looping around me, holding me in its field. They've cast a spell on me like ospreys do with fish, and I'm frozen. I cannot move. Everything settles into the waves and grooves of the land—wind, leaves, grasses—until there's only the wolves and me and the straight line between us. And that line becomes taut and it pulls me in, rounds out my edges like a gravitational force imposing the smallest, tightest shape possible on an orbiting moon: a sphere. I feel myself getting small, moving toward them—and then suddenly I snap awake as if from a dream, and I take a few steps backward, toward the quarry, straight and erect like the wolves. I walk backwards, up to the crest of a small hill of grasses, and only then do I turn my back. I'm over the hill and out of their sight—but they are still watching. I know they are still watching.

* * *

The new Syrian family has arrived. I go to Jedediah's office for a briefing. He is sitting at his desk, head in hands, brow fussed up. There are a few older children at the counter making bubbles with a pipette, one bubble inside the other, and a rainbow is threaded through the bubbles. They shout every time a bubble pops.

"Please, sit down," Jed says when I come in. He points to a chair, a red velvet thing that clashes with the lime walls. I sit.

"What did the note say?" I ask. "The note from Mohammad?"

"Oh. Right. It said: *There is a friend that sticks closer than a brother.*"

"That's beautiful."

"Yes. It's a proverb, from the Tanakh. He must have taken great care in finding it for me." He pauses for a moment, thoughtful, then darkens, like a storm is passing through. "Look. There's a few things you need to know about our new family."

"Okay."

"The father was killed in the war; the grandmother has cancer. The family won't admit this out loud; they ... they won't speak it. They gloss over it. They say she's not well. They won't say the word *cancer* and won't allow doctors to say it; they don't want to startle the grandmother. So. There's a grandmother, a mother with her son, and three brothers."

"Huh? Whose three brothers?"

"One grandmother. One daughter, three sons. Grandson, son of the daughter."

"Oh."

The children begin to shout. "Ha, ha! Look! Look!" They've created four bubbles, one inside the other.

Jed nods his head. "Aren't they brilliant?" he says to me.

"How does that work?" I ask him.

"Well, let's see. Well, bubbles use a minimum amount of surface area to enclose the volume of air trapped inside. When you blow the inner bubble, the fixed volume of the air in the *outer* bubble becomes, well, it is compressed by the growing *inner* bubble. The additional air not only causes the creation of the inner bubble, but it forces the outer bubble to expand to accommodate the inner bubble's volume. Do you understand?" He doesn't wait for an answer. He begins to speak more rapidly.

"Because of the soapy, sugary solution that the kids are using, the hydrogen bonds in the water are elastic enough to allow for the increase in volume and compression. Isn't that something? And also, the ... the bubble lasts longer on a surface that's free of oil or dirt particles that break through and dissolve the soap film. But it's gravity—*gravity*, that is a bubble's worst enemy: Gravity moves the film and water in the bubble downward, so the film gets thinner and thinner on top and finally can't hold together." He stops, finally.

"Okay. Wow. I wasn't looking for a physics lecture."

"Chemistry, actually."

"Gravity? That's chemistry? So what about the colours? Where do the colours come from? In one sentence."

"Can anyone answer that for Sarah?" Jed asks the kids. "Where do the colours on the bubbles come from?"

A few of them wave their arms vigorously. "I know, I know!" They jostle for Jed's attention.

"Amos, what do you think?"

Gladys' son Amos stands erect like a penguin with his little belly poking out from his track suit. "Like a rainbow!"

"That's it, Amos. It's like ... it's like the way we perceive colours in a rainbow. Or in an oil slick on water. We see the colours because of the reflection and refraction of light waves off the film surfaces of the bubble; the wavelengths of light are—well, they're mixing after they leave the surface of the bubble."

"Interesting. Can we get back to the Syrians?"

"Yes, of course. Well, the grandson—he's a teenager. Eighteen—but he looks older. His name is Hussein. He is autistic, and he wanders around a lot. But here's the thing ... " He pauses, searches for words. "Hussein has been—well, how do I say this. I'm not too sure how you will feel about this."

"For God's sake, just say it."

"Well, okay—he's been indoctrinated into radical Islamic teaching. He will often, I'm afraid, he will interrupt your class with threats from the Quran. He detests the West. Luckily, you won't know what he is saying. His English—he doesn't really have any English. He doesn't want to *learn* English. His mother, Fatima, has told him that we're Russian. So he likes us."

"Russian?"

"He seems to have an affinity for Russia."

"Okay. But why do we need Hussein to like us? Isn't *he* the one who is supposed to fit in?"

"Sar-ah. He is here. We can't change that. Let's do our best." He twists a pen between his fingers—a slender black fountain pen with a golden nib.

"And the mother. She's a good cook, fussy about what she eats, so I have alerted Mohammad and Haya. We will try to buy organic vegetables."

"*Organic*? She's a refugee. Even *I* can't afford organic."

"They come from wealth, Sarah. They've lost everything."

In my classroom, the students are waiting. The new family is there, sitting apart. Three men, an old woman, a younger woman—tall, bleached blond hair with dark roots, a bit of a stoop. Stained teeth, chipped. Glass beads around her neck. There's also the teenaged boy, tall and thin like a reed. And there's a baby. Jed didn't tell me about a baby. I don't ask why. Why there is a gap between the children; why the family is such an odd mixture. I put on my Canadian smile and greet them, ask a few questions.

"No English," the old woman says, her eyes stony.

"I speak," one of the brothers says. He's about thirty years old.

"Oh. Well. Can you translate for your family? Because my Arabic—I'm still working on it."

"Speak Arabic?"

"Yes. Try me."

He smiles. He knows that I know nothing of his world: a glimpse at the news, a few photographs and headlines are enough. The paradoxes of his culture and people and history are to me unfathomable, beyond understanding, and he senses my indifference.

I ask the family several questions to test their English. Only the one brother, whose name is Rasool, I discover, can converse in English. The others speak with groans and jolts like a broken-down mine car. But they are fluent in three other languages.

"What's your name?" I ask the younger woman. Just then, Hussein bolts out of his chair and begins to shout in Arabic, strutting in formation like a soldier, back and forth across the room, slapping his chest with each syllable. I'm appalled. Not fearful—just appalled and uneasy. I don't want him here.

His mother rushes to him.

"Shhhh, shhhh," she says. She reaches up and touches his hair, tries to soothe him, tries to get him to sit down.

"Her name Fatima," Rasool says.

"Did you come from Syria to Canada?" I try to ignore Hussein and the drama he is creating. The other students, seated around me, don't seem distracted. They behave as though nothing out of the ordinary is happening. They lean in, listen to my conversation above Hussein's shouting.

"Syria … Turkey … Canada."

"Ah, I see. Toronto first?"

"No."

"I see."

Hussein has quieted down. He is still marching, but he is quiet. I don't want him here. Fatima stands beside him, sapped, with a look of quiet desperation on her face. The old woman sits in the recliner. She wears a heavy black drape and black gloves. She looks like a gigantic bat girded with wings. Oblong bifocals are perched on the bridge of her nose, and she watches me over the glasses with an indifference that unnerves me. I try to draw a few more students into the conversation.

"Haya, how many children does Fatima have?" I want to move her into the third person point of view, using words like *he* and *she* instead of *you, I*, and *me*. I want her to say, *She has one child.*

"One," Haya says.

"Right. Okay. Um, let's try, *I've got peace like a river.*" I sing the song, using motions for *peace* and *river*.

"Mohammad, try it."

"I got piss like a river! I got piss like a river!"

I'm not going to fight it today. I lead the class through some talk about countries of origin, family, food. Anything but war and violence. Refugees by definition have stockpiles of trauma. Then they come into a wide, open space—Canada—and have difficulty learning. Everything they know, all of their social artefacts—quiet conversations, familiar streets, bustling markets, the sounds and tastes and aromas of their food—huddled together into one life like horses on a winter field—all have dispersed.

And now there is nothing to hold onto. Nothing to contextualize their learning. Because when you learn a word—say, *unrealistic*—it comes inside a series of bubbles—bubbles that *mean* something to you. You understand from an English grammar bubble that *-un* is a prefix denoting the absence of a quality or state, that *-ic* changes a noun into an adjective, and that *-ist* denotes the adherence to a system of beliefs. You know that you must get inside the word, to its source, *real*—another bubble—and that word has mathematical and philosophical and social meanings: something akin with being true or actual. And then, the word has another bubble: a deeply personal meaning with a life and memories.

But when all the bubbles pop and all the meaning evaporates, you find yourself reaching back, trying to find the pipette that holds the past within the present. But it is banging around somewhere just beyond the hollows of your mind, and you can't get a hold of it. And only emotions remain. So how do you learn? Music. Music fills the inner bubble, causes it to expand, and binds itself up with what remains: emotion. It brings right and left brain together in perfect harmony and ultimately, in healing.

* * *

At the end of class, I say goodbye to the new family, and Hussein sidles up to me. He smiles, says something in Arabic, then bends over and kisses me on the cheek.

"Get the hell *away* from me!" I screech, stepping backwards. Right then, Jed pops his head into the classroom.

"Hussein!" he says sternly.

Hussein smiles and begins walking in circles, gesticulating wildly with his hands.

"He doesn't mean anything by it," Jed says to me. "He's quite affectionate."

I try to control the groundswell of anger within me. "I will *not* teach with that guy in my classroom. I will *not*."

I pack up my briefcase and begin stacking chairs, slamming them on top of each other. The remaining students are suspended for a few moments, then they take off like a swirl of waxwings. Jed picks up some chairs and stacks them neatly and noiselessly.

"I need to speak with you about something," he says as we work. "May I come to your home this evening?"

I drop two chairs on a stack and turn toward him. "My *house*? You want to come to my *house*?"

"Yes."

"Can't we talk here?"

"No."

Why does he want to come to my house? To fire me for the way I treated Hussein? Suddenly all of my frustration, all of my anger, breaks up into a singular reality: I cannot afford to be jobless.

I give him directions. I don't give the address; I give the signs, embedded in the landscape and easier to follow: Cows at first, black and brown, and bales of hay and land so flat and aloof that it would recede from view apart from the mountains whip-stitched along its edges, mountains with beauty so startling, so unrehearsed against the cerulean sky that you are stripped of every alibi, every plea. Go to them. Go through the Stoney Reserve, through the misshapen houses sinking into the landscape in arbitrary places with porch lights on in the daytime, little lights dotting the pall of fields with horses uncorralled and unharnessed. Yamnuska is the first mountain you will see, its flat face renowned among rock climbers. City people think Yamnuska means "big chief" because it looks like a chief lying on his back, his prominent nose sniffing up the sky. But in the Stoney language, the word sounds more like E-am-nuth-ka and means something like "boy with loose strands of hair." That's why the mountain is popular among climbers, I suppose; they hang onto the strands of hair.

When you pass Yamnuska, the mountains will come upon you suddenly. They will flank you and wrap themselves around you like a woman wraps herself around a man, and you will be *inside* them; inside a conspiracy of beauty that feels like a heavy load being lifted from your arms, leaving them weightless and rubbery. The road will turn like the weather does, and you'll see Heart Mountain and Ha Ling Peak. Ha Ling will guide you, sometimes standing before you, sometimes beside you, always in your sightline, pointing the way through the passage like the cloud leading the Israelites. You'll see Big Sister, then all three Sisters, named by a mountaineer who saw their veils of snow in the early morning and called them nuns, but then bits of his story began to pool like pockets of warm air do and the nuns became Sisters—Faith, Hope, and Charity—and later, Big Sister, Middle Sister, and Little Sister. And it's been said that you haven't really visited these mountains until you've summited one of the Sisters—Middle Sister, likely, because Big Sister is unremitting and Little Sister unruly.

Soon Mount Rundle will straddle the road, awash in glory and taking you to a place beyond the murmurs of the Cree fathers who named it first, named it *Waskahigan Watchi*, or *House Mountain*. You'll see an open area with elk, a large herd, probably, and finally, Miner's peak, tied to Ha Ling with a fold of skin in the rock, and together the two peaks look like breasts of an old woman, hanging down and pulling away from each other. Then woods, and three trees standing apart like wardens. The quarry is there. My house, pale yellow like winter grasses, is beside the quarry.

"You sound like you're in love," he says.

"Be careful," I respond. "Don't get out of the car. Lots of wolves and bears …"

He frowns.

"I'm kidding. But don't feed the bunnies."

"What bunnies?"

"Domesticated bunnies living wild. Lots of them."

He raises his chin a little, says nothing. His eyes have dark lines under them, dark passings like coal seams.

"The bunnies—they draw in predators, you know. Cougars and wolves watching the kids on the playground."

On the drive home, my thoughts are high-pitched. Why is he coming over? Because I snapped at Hussein? Will I lose my job? What have I done? A truck with a long trailer pulls up beside me, tries to pass. The trailer has small slots, and I see an eye looking out of one of the slots, a solitary eye with darkness behind it. We ride beside each other for a while, through fields of wheat and barley, then waves of canola, and then avocado bluffs and the slate green of the foothills. Finally, the driver relents and falls back into the deep sky and the shallows in the road.

I come to the quarry and pull into my driveway, hard to spot even now, even now with the evergreens so high and hard-packed. Inside, my house is small, piled up with books and trinkets like an osprey nest. I don't clean much. Filth and grime is pressed into the corners, and I can't get it out. Sometimes my father used to come over, scrub at it, bent over like van Gogh's peasant women in the peat fields, cleaning baseboards with a toothbrush. But the grime always came back. So what was the point?

I fix myself some licorice tea and Kraft Dinner with sliced tomatoes on top and get a book. *Alice in Wonderland*. Alice going underground and finding things, like a miner. On the front deck is a small metal table with Moroccan tiles and two matching chairs with tiny cushions, faded and flat from the weather. I sit down, open my book, and watch the ravens soar above the trees in acrobatic flight. In Yellowknife, ravens perch on supermarket rooftops and push snow on people who pass underneath. Jedediah is nothing like that.

The sun sets early in the mountains, and soon after dark Jed pulls up in an old station wagon, gets out of the car. He steps onto the porch and looks around. The eaves are plugged with needles and leaves, and in the corners are thick cobwebs with squat spiders letting out silk and eating it up again.

"May I sit?" he asks.

"Of course. Want some tea?"

"No," he says brusquely, then: "No, thank you." Softer this time. He examines the insects in the spider webs, wrapped up like mummies. His nose is hooked up high at the bridge, and he sniffs once or twice.

"Well," he finally says.

I wait. It's dark, and there's no wind.

"Well, I came here to tell you that I—I'm going to Israel. To live. My father is there. He has a house—well, like, a place of refuge. For widows and orphans. I'm going to live with him."

"You're leaving The Booth?"

"I want to go home, Sarah. The Jews are returning to Israel. From Turkmenistan and—well, from all over. Ethiopia. Russia. I want to go back and help my people. Many of them are like—like refugees. They aren't accepted because they aren't Israelis. They are Jewish, but they aren't Israeli-born."

"Oh."

"I want you to come with me."

"What?"

"To Israel. I want you to come to Israel."

"What are you talking about? You want me to come there and work?"

"Yes. *No!* No … not exactly."

"What are you talking about?"

"Sarah." He looks at me, his eyes deep and reflective like the quarry. And then I know. The backs of my legs begin to tingle. And it feels like I've always known. Like I've always known something was there, but I didn't have the words to bring it into being.

I wait for him to speak. To say it.

"Sarah. I want you to be where I am."

"I thought … I thought you were coming here to fire me."

His eyes wrinkle up and he laughs out loud, big belly laughs. It's the first time I've seen him abandon himself.

"Want to go for a walk?" I ask. "In the woods?"

He looks out at the night.

"I have headlamps. We'll be like miners." We get the headlamps from the house and walk to the quarry, and the light from our lamps cuts up the trail, shows us the way.

"Turn off your lamp," I say after a while. It's dark and quiet and the stars are opening. When we turn off the lamps, we see eyes in the darkness, across Quarry Lake—a black wall punctured by little ghosts of light.

"A herd of elk, I think."

"Oh my!" Jed says. "Let's go see!" He lunges through the tufts of dry grass, and I follow, the light from my headlamp ricocheting against the bumps and rivets of the land.

"Slow down," I say. "Be quiet, or we'll scare them."

The grasses flatten out all around us, and then we see them. At least twenty. The trees behind them are tall and dark, and we huddle together like the elk. The minutes fuse together in holy matrimony, and it feels like all of the groaning, all of the longing, all of the birth pangs of Earth have ceased for this moment. I nod at Jed and we skirt around the elk and move into the woods. And in the darkness the trees begin to move, bending to the rhythm of Vincent's paints and bringing Heaven and Earth together like Jacob's ladder.

"I feel at home in the woods," I say quietly.

"Why is that?"

"They comfort me, I guess. Sometimes when you stand on the outskirts of a wood, you're afraid. You don't know what's waiting inside. But then, when you pass over that threshold of fear, you find treasures."

"Ancient pathways. Waiting to be revealed."

"Yeah. Something like that. You know, there's a shelter in here. With a memorial. Last year, a boy gathered some sticks and branches and made a shelter and went inside and killed himself. Sometimes I go there. But the shelter is empty. It feels so empty."

We are quiet for a while.

"Like an empty tomb," Jed says. "The shelter."

"Kind of. I don't think anyone goes inside it. It's holy ground."

I stand tall like the trees.

"Look, Jed, about what you said. About Israel. I'm German. You know, Mennonite? *Not Jewish.*" I pick up a strand of my hair and hold it under his eyes—it's waxy white like hairs on a cob of corn. He leans over, strokes the thin strand of hair with his fingertips, then pulls his hand away.

"My parents—you know, the older generation—there's a lot of shame. And even I—even people my age have had to come to terms with what happened. We weren't even born yet, but we still carry the guilt. And I guess—I don't know. I don't know why I'm telling you this. It's not the reason, really. I just don't think I can leave this place."

"Sarah, my father's house has many rooms. Let me get one ready for you. Then come for a little while. Come for a visit. See how you like it. See how you like … me."

"We've only worked together for—for how long? I don't know. You're my boss. You don't even know me."

"I've always known you." He is standing close, watching me.

"Where in Israel?"

"Jerusalem. Close to the Old City."

"Are you hungry?"

"Yeah."

"Want some eggs?"

"Okay."

We thread our way back to the house. The front door is coming off the hinges, so I lift it up and open it gingerly.

"Got a screw driver?" Jed asks. "I can fix that."

"Nope."

We take off our shoes and jackets, and Jed's feet are bare.

"Don't you own any socks?"

"Nope."

He's wearing a black button down and baggy black jeans. He looks like Johnny Cash.

We go into the kitchen, and I take out eggs and a frying pan.

"Let me do it," he says.

"Don't trust my cooking?"

He doesn't respond. He cracks the eggs into the pan, scrambles them, adds salt and pepper. I put out rye bread and crabapple jelly, and we eat.

"Tell me about Turkmenistan."

"You mean the Turkmen Jews? Well, they have no semblance of a community now. The majority are non-practicing."

"Why?"

"Because. Severe persecution. They can't even disclose their religious origin. Sunni Islam and the Russian Orthodox Church are the only legal religions in Turkmenistan. All other denominations are forbidden to have a place of worship. Surveillance cameras are everywhere—they're in all the public places. Turkmenistan is the only country in Central Asia whose government *sponsors* religious persecution and anti-Semitism."

"So that's why they're leaving."

"Yes. More than 2,000 since the collapse of the Soviet Union. And those left behind are in a precarious situation, you know? No Jewish community, Islamic fundamentalism on the rise, human rights violations, and the media is of course government-controlled. Foreigners can't even walk the streets after dark. Political parties have been—well, banned, and—and opposition leaders are in jail. It's a dangerous place for Turkmen Jews— more repressive than any other place in the region. So most of them have fled. And the ones who are still there? Their sole occupation is getting the money and documentation they need to get out—to get to Israel."

"How many are left?"

"No more than 1,200. But half the world doesn't even know they exist. It's a forgotten community, isolated from world Jewry."

"Wow. It's so different from here."

"Not so different. It's coming, Sarah. It's already here. But it's unseen. It's underground. Do you know what most communities say after they have been subsumed by an enemy?"

"I don't want to hear this."

"They say, we never thought it would happen to *us*. We never thought it would come *here*."

I change the subject. "When are you leaving?"

"Three weeks."

"What about the home? The Booth?"

"A new director has been assigned."

"Are there any mountains there? In Israel?"

"Sar-ah. I know this sounds … unexpected. But, I, I feel—well, I've given it a lot of thought. I'm asking you to, to consider it."

"What colour?" I ask. "What colour would my room be?"

He looks around, looks at the peeling paint on the windowsill and streaks of mud and rain on the glass.

"Brown. Muddy brown."

"I like brown. I'll think about it."

* * *

For the next three weeks, I'm numb. All the colours in the kaleidoscope have shifted. I move between the quarry and The Booth, averting my eyes from the kill sites along the highway—dead deer with murders of crows hopping on their bodies in a frenzied dance, delirious by the blood and meat.

I catch glimpses of Jed in the hallways and in his office, and the images linger, stay with me as I walk the quarry and hike Ha Ling. I watch him with the students and see his affection breaking out like spring crocuses. On rare occasions, I see him passing by my classroom door, spirit-like, glimpsing in. And I wonder if I still belong to the world of incontrovertible fact. I wonder if I've been wrong about Jed: He's like the woods, certainly—aloof and meditative, inscrutable—but he's loose, too, like ravens mating in a complex dance of chases, dives, and rolls, their songs more varied and artful and evocative than any other bird calls—expressing tenderness, happiness, surprise, and rage.

But he's Jewish. He's returning to Israel, to his father's house. How could I live in another country, under someone else's roof?

As the day of his departure comes in close, I avoid him. But on the Monday, four days before he is scheduled to leave, he sees me in the hallway and calls me into his office. There's a knot of children surrounding the ant farm, watching them build tunnels. Jed is teaching them.

"Ant colonies are kind of like human communities," he tells them. "They have complex societies … a rigid division of labour. Massive populations, just massive—and unified—they have rules. Rules about eating, reproducing, waging war—they are masters of war. And if … if anyone breaks the rules, they are punished."

"They don't understand a word you're saying."

"How do *you* know what they understand?" He sits down behind his desk, pulls his hair back into a ponytail, rakes his beard with his fingers. I sit across from him, look around at his office. It's in a state of complete disarray: piles of paper and books and beakers and maps everywhere. There's a small plant on his desk, a Crown of Thorns, with tiny red flowers supported by petal-like bracts. A beautiful plant, but mildly poisonous. Makes you vomit if you eat it.

Jed asks the kids to leave and closes the door.

"It looks like my living room in here," I say.

"Have you thought about it?"

I draw in a breath, let it out slowly. "I think, I think it's just too much for me, Jed. I've lived alone for so long, you know? I'm comfortable."

"I know." He pauses for a moment, folds his hands in his lap. "They want English, you know."

"Who does?"

"The Jews who are coming home. My father knows many of them. They want to learn English."

"What's your father's name? What does he do?"

"His name is David. He was a physician before he retired."

"And your mother?"

"She passed away when I was young. She was a Ukrainian Jew. Hid in the caves during the war."

"What caves?"

"The caves in—well, western Ukraine was a brutal place for Jews. Almost all of them were killed. My grandfather—my mother's father—he knew that if his family went to a concentration camp, it would be … it would be certain death. So when the Germans … when the Germans came to round up the Jews, he took his family and ran. They ran to a man they knew who lived in the woods. The man brought them to a hole in the ground in a field that he knew about. That hole led to a series of underground tunnels and caves the size of this room, I think. They hid there for five hundred days."

"Five hundred days? How did they survive?"

"The men slipped out of the hole at night, scavenged for food and clothing where they could. Cut wood for fire. That was the most dangerous part, because it was noisy in the middle of the night. The women and children waited in the cave, not knowing if the men would return.

My mother—she developed night terrors. She was paralyzed with fear. I don't think she ever recovered."

"Oh. I'm sorry."

"Once when they were cutting wood, a townsman appeared in the woods. Someone they had been neighbours with. And they had to decide what to do. Should they kill him? They decided to let him go. That evening, he came to the hole with the townsmen, and they began to shoot at my family."

"How did they know where the hole was?"

"I'm not sure. I don't know how well known the caves were. But they began to shoot into the hole, and my uncle put a big boulder in front of the hole. Saved their lives. After that, they couldn't leave the caves. For three months, they slept and lived off the few rations they had. And then freedom came."

"What happened?"

"The strangest thing. When they came out of the caves and went into the town, none of their neighbours came out to greet them. They stayed in their houses. So I guess—I guess my mother's family never did get out of those caves. They were still invisible, still underground."

"Jed, do you understand how impossible it would be for me to be—you know … herded into a little room in your father's house when—I mean, you've seen where I live."

"Yes. You are like a wild animal, Sarah."

"You sound like my father," I say tersely.

"Sarah, I didn't mean—I meant it as a compliment. You're wild, like the land. That's what—that's why … well, land that is wild is—is unresolved. Nonpartisan. It's open. Open to be explored." He takes the gold earring out of his ear and holds it out to me. "Please. Take this. It was my mother's wedding band. I had it crafted into an earring."

"What? I can't take that."

"Please." He walks around the desk and kneels beside me. He unwraps my fisted hand and places the ring in my palm. It is gold, studded with bits of silver like eyes on a wheel, and between the silver studs are three tiny black pearls, deeply imbedded like a small seam of coal, blue-black in the darkness.

I stand up. "I can't go with you. I really can't." I look away from the ripples in his face and walk outside to my Jeep, the ring still in my hand. I drive through the foothills to the mountains and I see horses, blue against green-gold grasses. At home, I drop the ring into a small bowl beside the telephone where I keep keys and loose change. I walk to the kitchen window, sit down, then stand up again, restless like a gust of mountain wind. I pick up Jed's ring, press it between my fingers, then try to push it through a piercing in my ear. The hole has grown over—I haven't worn earrings since I was a teenager. I poke the earring through the skin, feel its weight. It stings.

I need to get outside. There's a narrow path outside my back door that leads through the woods and up to Grassi Lakes. I take the path, wind my way up to the lakes. They are clear and green and lovely with reflections so clean that the lakes themselves disappear, like messages in an icon. But they are mountain lakes, born of snow—impossible to swim in. The rock face on the opposite side has deep, deep pores, because at one time, it was a shallow-water ocean reef. Over time, the reef material was replaced with calcium, and rock was born—but the rock maintains the reef structure of the past—can't let it go.

A few climbers are scaling the rock face like ants. In a small cave above them an owl stands, watching as a climber approaches on an adjacent line, his yellow clothing freckled against the grey rock. The climber reaches back for chalk, dusts his fingers. He bends with the rock and moves closer to the owl. The owl is still, perfectly still. There are chicks inside that cave, maybe. Intuitively, I reach up and press Jed's earring between my fingers, twist it around and around. I take it out and look at it. It's green-gold like the lakes. The climber moves past the owl, above the cave, and the owl, grey like the rock, disappears into the icon. I think of Jed. Will he call me, ask me to reconsider, or will he disappear like the owl?

* * *

And then the day comes. Friday. Jed comes into my classroom, and the students are listless: They know he has come to say goodbye. He sits down, crosses his legs and arms, says nothing. No one speaks. The chickadees on the windowsill have eaten all the seeds I put out for them. I am on edge; I don't know what to say.

Mohammad wheels up to Jed and places a great big hand on either side of Jed's head, his thick fingers all over Jed's face. He leans in and presses his forehead against Jed's forehead, and he begins to weep. Haya too weeps quietly in her chair, and the students are silent and watchful. And I wonder if Mohammad knows that Jed is Jewish. Because I can see that Mohammad and Jedediah love each other with a violent love, a fearful and holy love, wrapped around each other like Arabic letters. The other students come closer, all except Hussein and the old woman; they remain in their seats. But the others gather around him and he covers them with his arms like a hen covers her chicks.

"How I long for you," he whispers. "How I long for you."

I look out the window, look for the chickadees, but the ledge is bare. I'm conflicted, filled up with blackness like the coal mines.

* * *

Later, at home, there is darkness, and the answering machine is blinking on and off like dawn coming over a hill. I press the play button. There's a long pause, then Jed.

"Sarah? I will come back for you. The earring. From my mother. It's a promise. It's a ... a covenant. I will come back. You will hear about wars and rumours of wars in the Middle East. Don't be afraid. I will come back. Don't be afraid. Sarah? I ... I ... " And then his voice is cut off. I don't understand the message at all. Wars and rumours of wars? Why did he say that? War is not new. The whole world is at war.

I walk outside, to the quarry. A fog is brooding over the water and seagulls are hovering, appearing and disappearing like little pearls in the ashen sky. An osprey is building a nest at the top of a fir tree, coming and going with branches and grasses. I think about Jed's message. Why would I be afraid? I'm not. I live in Canada. It's as if Jed knows something. It's as if he knows that a storm is coming.

Act Four: Pentecost

(SHAVU'OT) — SIVAN (MAY-JUNE)

On Monday, he's gone. I go to The Booth, and he's gone. My classroom feels like a reclaimed mine: stripped of its jewels, then filled in and walked over. We're all there, but we're hollowed out. The students are sitting in a circle, talking quietly.

Gladys stands and addresses me. "Sarah, I will sing. In Swahili."

She begins to sway and dance, lifting her hands up to Heaven. I sit down to watch, and then my heart stops dead by a yelp—a bellow of unspeakable pain. It's Gladys. She falls to her knees, hides her face in her hands. The others are rigid and silent. And then, Gladys erupts into terrible, exulted laughter.

I am appalled. "Gladys? Why are you laughing?"

"He's gone, gone, gone. Gone with the wind, they say." Then she begins to sing on her knees in silvery Swahili. A love song, I think.

How? How does she sing? Her entire family was murdered in front of her eyes in South Sudan. After she came to The Booth with little Amos, she found an apartment. Then she met two African men, let them move in with her. And they began to beat her, and now she's back at The Booth.

"Why did you put yourself and Amos in danger like that?" I had asked her.

"It's the African way, Sarah."

"But this isn't South Sudan, Gladys. The government will take Amos away from you. Do you understand? They will take your child if you put him in jeopardy. Do you understand me? This is not South Sudan."

"Just a little slip, Sarah. Just a little slip."

And now, she's moving with the song. The song is interceding for her, I think; mediating her pain. Mediating all of our pain.

Esperance begins to speak in Swahili, pointing at her legs. She is wearing a long cotton tunic with pants underneath.

"Do you need more pants?" I ask. She looks exasperated and repeats herself.

"She's asking you if she is required to wear a tunic in Canada," Gladys says with a sigh, coming back to the circle of students, rubbing her eyes and her face. "She wants to know if it's okay for a woman to wear pants without a tunic."

"Sure, Esperance. Look at *me*." I point to my clothing: boyfriend jeans with holes and a faded t-shirt.

The students laugh a little. They are well-dressed and formal. I wonder what they must think of me, deep down. But I won't change the way I do things. Not in my own country. We exchange a few words, and then there is silence. We are sluggish, muted, staring.

A short, balding woman hustles into the classroom.

"You are Sarah?" she asks me. This must be Jed's replacement.

"Yes. Are you the new director?"

"I am. I am Olga. I came Saturday." She extends her hand.

"So nice to meet you." We shake hands, and she straightens her back a little.

"Sarah, please come to my office when you're finished teaching."

"Sure." I detect an eastern European accent. "Where are you from?"

"What? I am Canadian!"

"But where were you born? Where are you from originally? I can hear an accent."

She scowls a little and lifts her chin, rounded out with large pores like raindrops in the snow.

"Accent is good. People say, why you have accent? You been here thirty-four years. I say, my accent, it's *beautiful!* Ridiculous, getting rid of accent! *Why?* We are all Canadian. But I answer your question: Russia. I'm from Russia."

* * *

After class, I go to Olga's office, to Jed's office, and look in: The books are all in the bookcase—not on the floor. The walls have been painted grey, and the periodic table has been replaced by abstract art in metal frames. The ant colony is in the hallway.

"This is more modern. I prefer modern," Olga says when I come in. "And there's no lock on my apartment! Can you believe it? They installing locks tomorrow. And that *stupid* ant farm! Those ants escape, we have big, big problem. *Stupid.* Hardwood coming next week. The carpet *filthy*. And those magpies outside, making racket! Like my relatives. Charlie? *Charlie!* Come in here!"

A young man in white coveralls hustles into the room, a little stiff in the torso.

"Charlie, get the pellet gun. Get rid of those damn *magpies!*"

Charlie nods his head and hustles out.

"Now. Sarah. Tell me about your class."

I'm stiffening up like Charlie. "Well, I come in at one, typically. Teach for … "

"No good. You must come in earlier, when students fresh. What do you teach?"

"Well … I, I teach English."

"I know *that*. What you teaching them *right now?*" She looks me up and down, looks at my Birkenstocks and the mustard stain on my t-shirt.

"Well … the students are all at different levels … it's difficult … "

"Yes, yes. Is difficult. I know that."

" … so we sing a lot. The singing is therapeutic."

"But they must learn *English*. Why you not teaching them *English?*"

I'm getting a little hot around the ears. "I *am* teaching them English. Every song has vocabulary, grammar, sentences. The beginners learn the words. Advanced students, I teach them proper grammar and pronunciation. Then after the lesson we have conversation and tea … "

"*Tea?* Why you need *tea* in *English* class? You don't need *tea!*" Her voice sounds like a rusted-out hinge on an old door, rising in pitch at the height of her sentences.

A pellet gun goes off outside, several crisp shots. I jump in my seat.

"Okay, Sarah. I have too much to do. I see you tomorrow."

* * *

The next morning, I'm frantic to find something to wear. I rifle through my closet, but it offers only quick-dry hiking clothes, fleeces, t-shirts, and jeans. The hiking pants are beige like dress pants, so I put them on with a long-sleeved tee. I arrive at The Booth at 11 a.m., and Olga is in the classroom. The students are seated in rows of tables and chairs, writing down English letters and words. The old woman is in the recliner, and Hussein is marching, his arms and his face stiff.

"Sarah. Good. You are here. Your students *must* write from left to right. Do you see how they make letters?"

She is standing above Fatima. "Please. Draw a 't'."

Fatima moves her pencil from top to bottom, constructing the post, then from right to left to make a cross. Olga taps her knuckles with a pen.

"No. Like this."

She takes the pencil and makes the cross from left to right.

"Now you try."

Fatima makes the cross from left to right.

"It's the same," I say. "It looks exactly the same. What difference does it make ... "

"They *must* do it correctly." She raises her voice to a sharp pitch. "Sarah, you are not *teaching* them! You *must* teach spelling and grammar. *Please*."

I am dumbfounded. She is chastising me in front of my students. But the students don't seem bothered. They are busily constructing letters and words, and I wonder if the rote learning so frowned upon in the West is, in fact, more conducive to learning. I wonder if perhaps I have imposed Western constructs on essentially Eastern ways of knowing—if my teaching is too foreign, too *other*. I wonder if I'm like a bee bumping up against a window pane, never able to get through.

Hussein, of course, cannot draw the letters. He moves toward Olga, his shoulders bobbing up and down like an invisible string is pulling on them, and he drums on his chest with his fingers. Olga smiles at him.

"He like Russians," she says to me. "He don't like the West. This country. English is crazy language. Example. Last night, I go to Safeway. There was immigrant standing outside. I say to him: 'Why you standing outside?' 'I need coffee,' he says, 'only coffee. But sign says I must buy twelve items!'" Olga roars in laughter, and the ridges in her face take on tones of purple.

"I can tell you so many stories, Sarah. *So* many stories! So hard to immigrate to new country. When I first came, I took English class. At end of class, teacher come to my desk. 'See you later,' she said to me. *See you later?* What does that *mean*? In Russian, we say, see you tomorrow. Or see you in an hour. See you *later*? What does that mean? I sat for an hour. Waited for her to come back! Crazy language."

"Then why do you stay here? If it's so difficult?"

She appraises me for a moment. I don't care. I'm angry. Don't criticize my country.

"Refugees not what they used to be. Now, they don't work. When I came, I work *hard* to make a life here. Now, they know about welfare before they come."

Olga knows nothing about The Booth, I think. The refugees are *compelled* to work, *compelled* to survive because they have a common enemy, deep underground—failure, collapse, destruction—I don't know what it is, exactly. But it breeds in them a primordial hunger to survive. No sentiment can overpower it—no joy or pride or terror or despair or shame or courage or fury—all are grass that withers in noonday sun. No religion, no beliefs, no doctrines can satisfy it. Survival depends—for now—not on theories and principles and canons, but on solidarity. And so the refugees—like Jed's ants—have become a colony. The Arabs shop and cook and serve meals; the African men maintain the building, keep it oiled; the African women care for the children, scrub and clean. And only now do I realize how imperative Jed's presence was. His steady, calm presence among a people ravaged by violence and chaos, defiled by dark thoughts and brute fatalism.

"Government just keeps bringing them in. Bring them in! Don't care how much overtime I do! Don't know *nothing* about who's coming in."

"The government does background checks. You know that."

"How? *How?* So naïve! I tell you story." She lowers her voice, stands close so the students won't hear. "A lady come here to escape torture in Middle East. Government gave her apartment. Few weeks after she moved in, she found her torturer living in same building! Can you believe it? Canadians? Sooo *nice!* Such *nice* people. You know what? They think everyone else nice too. Canadians are *naïve.* Dull. Don't know nothing. Don't even *know* they being invaded."

The old woman in the recliner emits several deep glottal sounds and stretches out her neck. Olga looks at her for a moment, then continues.

"Jed, too. Just like those Jews in Hungary. They said, no one coming. No one touch us here. Too far away. Soon all of them in concentration camps."

I'm appalled. Are we like domesticated bunnies? Drawing in predators—or creating them, even, because it's too hard here? The weather, the language, the customs—even the *country* is hard. You have to *prove* that you're poor if you want to eat: You have to fill out forms, produce documents, tell lies. If you want a good job, you have to be educated in Canada—and before you can attend school you have to pass an English test—but the government is cutting higher-level English programs. So you work three jobs to pay the rent, and on your day off, you go to the food bank and the doctor and the shopping mall on the bus with your four children in sub-zero temperatures.

And then the veil comes down, and you realize that you cannot navigate the physical and social terrain here. I've heard about people on waiting lists for English classes, unable to get a job without English. Sitting in cold basement suites, dark thoughts finding them out, speaking things that they do not know, that they had not contemplated until they were knitted into this vast loneliness.

Olga turns to leave the room. "Okay. I have too much work to do. Teach them English. *Please.*"

I look at Fatima. She is constructing t's and m's and h's and d's, right to left. And I think about what Jed taught me about the Semitic region and the languages there—Hebrew, Arabic, Assyrian, and their parent language, Aramaic—and other languages like Azerbaijani, Yiddish, and Persian from closer regions. All of these languages were popularized with the use of stone tablets: The Ten Commandments were written on stone, and so was the Assyrian Flood Tablet that described an immense flood in the Middle East. When a right-handed person took a chisel and hammer to a stone, he held the chisel with his left hand and the hammer with his right—and he moved from right to left. And then eventually, Islam came into the Arabic script, and in Islam, the right hand is devoted to doing *right*eous things—eating, shaking hands, giving charity to others—so Muslims write from the right, because everything that starts from the right is honourable to them.

A young man enters the room. He's wearing a white chef's frock with fabric buttons and a yellowing collar. The sleeves are too short; they stop at his forearms.

"I am Paul," he says. "From Pakistan. I am the new cook."

"We don't need a cook. Mohammad and Haya do the cooking."

"No. Olga hired me. I started yesterday."

"Oh. But what will Mohammad and Haya do?"

"Olga says they have to learn English so they can find work. She says they do not have time to cook."

"They *are* learning English. From me. Besides—the kitchen is upstairs."

He points at the minifridge. "I am storing extra food here."

"But Mohammad and Haya buy the food. They know what everyone likes to eat."

"I will learn." He pauses for a moment. "Yesterday, I served noodles. I thought, we're in Canada. Canadians like noodles. But they would not eat. They would not *eat!* So I will cook what the people like. I am proud of my food."

Paul explains that he cooked at a high-end restaurant in Pakistan for fifteen years. Now he's flipping pancakes and pork sausages at Denny's when he's not at The Booth, and in his spare time, he attends a culinary school with hungover nineteen- and twenty-year-olds because he's a foreigner and he has an accent. He says that in culinary school, there are three streams: pastry chef, line cook, and butcher. "Butchering is good," he tells me. "Lots of work. Pays well."

"Then get a butcher job."

"I'm a cook."

"But you gotta pay the rent."

"I'm a cook."

"Why is your name Paul? You're from Pakistan."

"It's a nickname."

"Okay. Why is your nickname Paul?"

"Long story." He takes an armful of vegetables out of the fridge and begins chopping at one of the tables.

"Can't you do that upstairs? I'm trying to teach."

"Olga told me I must prepare food down here, then cook it upstairs."

"But why? That doesn't make any sense."

"The workers. They are modernizing the kitchen. Putting in new appliances. A gas stove, better for cooking. Bigger fridge and dishwasher."

"How can you cook with the workers there?"

"They will leave soon, I hope."

The students, sequestered in their table-and-chair ghettos, are bent over their letters, copying words and short sentences from workbooks that Olga has given them. I walk up and down the aisles like a lab rat in a maze, like my classroom has been subverted into some kind of scapegoat mechanism, and I've been sent into the wild, outside the camp.

Over the next several weeks, Olga hires childcare workers and cleaners, making the students' jobs redundant. They are no longer needed. They start to bicker and complain and hoard rations from the storage room. The Booth accumulates dirt and grime, because hired workers do not tend its corridors like someone who lives there. Olga insists that I follow a prescribed curriculum, that the students do two hours of homework each day. They spend more and more time in their rooms studying English syntax and grammar and watching television late into the night, sleeping through the mornings. And more disturbing is this: A line forms between Africans and Arabs, between Christians and Muslims.

They congregate in separate quarters, separate camps: African Christians on the deck, Muslim Arabs in the dining room.

"It's okay," Olga says. "If they study, it's okay. They *must* learn English. They *must* get job. If they don't get job, I get trouble. The buck stops with me. Always with me."

There is still a level of camaraderie in my classroom, I think, until one afternoon when I'm returning from coffee break. I enter the room, and there is an unusual silence. Even Hussein is sitting at the window, murmuring softly. The old woman has left early. I don't care, particularly. I don't want her here anyway. But why is everyone so rigid? I sit at my desk and watch. No one raises a hand, no one says a word. They look like gerberas, straight stems with heads nodding over their work. At the end of the class, they file out of the room, and I catch Mohammad by the arm.

"Mohammad, can I speak with you for a moment?"

"Yes."

I close the door after the others have left.

"Mohammad, what happened during coffee break?"

"Why you ask me this?"

"Because. It was so quiet."

"We plan celebration, Sarah. For Canada Day."

I'm relieved.

"But Sarah, planning not good. We want special colours, you know. Decorate classroom. Don de Dieu say, I want Congo colours. Syrians say, we want red stars. Sadya say, I want blue, and yellow stars. They yelling. It's a *shame*, I say to them. *Shame* on you! You bringing your fighting to this country, peaceful country open its arms, give us a home. Shame. So no party, Sarah. Sorry. No party."

"Why, Mohammad? It seems like the students are changing."

"Before, Shia, Sunni, Christian. All problems hidden. Dislikes hidden, not spoken out loud. They still there, just inside. Now, it comes out; if I hate you, I say it. Today, we said it. It came out."

I don't know what to do with a situation like this: Cultures, religions, and histories twisted into knots and transported into my classroom. I think about Jed, what he would do. I yearn for his presence of mind and quiet demeanour.

* * *

Sometimes a wolf will breed with a coyote, and a new creature emerges—a coywolf. Coyote skull with wolf teeth. You can feel them when you're in the woods. Sometimes you can hear them: a wolf's howl, deep in pitch, splintering into coyote yips. They came from Algonquin Park over one hundred years ago and moved like a brush fire across North America, filling in the hollows where wolves once roamed until the wolves were all but exterminated—the final solution to a population at once feared and misunderstood. Coywolves are hybrids of intellect and adaptability, thriving in country fields, suburbs and cities, golf courses, alleyways and backyards. They move into the creases of urban environments undetected, devouring docile prey like rats and geese and cats and fawns—skull and all—and docility, as always, gives way to totalitarianism. And the coywolves travel like the miners did, along the railways, the corridors that link lives together.

* * *

Outside The Booth in the back garden, domesticated bunnies are multiplying. The African children hop around with them while their parents sun themselves on the deck. Esperance is bent over her letters, the stub of a pencil pressed between her fingertips.

"Esperance, we just finished class. Take a rest," I say. Gladys translates for me.

"English bad," Esperance says. Her legs are spread open, supporting a rounded belly.

"No, no. You're really improving, right Gladys?"

Gladys grins. "You got it all, baby doll."

Esperance beams.

I look around the deck. Peeling paint and bits of garbage pressed between the wooden slats. It never used to look like this. The African men always kept it swept clean.

"I miss singing," Gladys says. "You remember, Sarah, *Hallelujah*?"

"*See you soon, see you soon,*" I sing.

"*Halleluuuuuuuuuujaaaaaah,*" Gladys sings, recounting our final song of the day when students held the notes as long as they could and erupted into laughter when I told them that they were not allowed to take a breath.

"And Jed. I miss him."

"Yes," I say. It's only been a few weeks, but when I think of him, images move through my mind like a thunder storm.

"Whenever it rained, he always came here," Gladys says. "He stood on the deck—sometimes he went out on the grass—and he just stood so still with his arms held out and his head up, like he was praying."

"Oh. I didn't know that."

"He loved the rain, right Esperance?" She speaks to Esperance in Swahili, and Esperance smiles, covers her mouth with her hand.

"But we, we don't like it. Too cold here when it rains. We stay inside."

"Gladys, I've noticed lately. The Africans and Arabs. They don't eat together anymore. They don't talk in the classroom."

"I think we are afraid."

"Afraid? Why?"

"You know what happens at night? When you and Olga are gone? The new family brings people in. People from outside. They come from the bad places."

"The bad places? You mean the other side of the river?"

"Yeah. They call it Warsaw. I don't know Warsaw. I don't know anything about it."

The city is divided into two parts: east and west of the river. West of the river is White, essentially, and the other side—the east side, is set apart from the decorum of the west like a Cartesian apartheid.

"We're afraid. The people that come, they are unkind to us. We stay in our rooms. But sometimes they stand outside and wait for us to come out. And they watch us. They just stand and watch us."

"Why don't you tell Olga?"

"Olga knows. She does nothing. Nothing."

She looks at the bunnies, and then her eyes widen. She bolts from her chair and rushes to the garden, shouting in Swahili, waving her hands. A coywolf is standing on the threshold of the yard. It stands still, watching the children. It is shaded and barely visible. Gladys rushes at it, clapping and shouting. The animal considers her, but doesn't move. Not until Esperance and I also run toward it does it turn and trot away. Gladys yells at the children.

"Come! Come! Come with me!" She gathers them up and hustles them inside, then returns to the deck.

Paul comes out, wiping his hands on his frock. "What's going on?"

"A wolf!" Gladys shouts.

"No. It wasn't a wolf," I say to Paul. "It was a hybrid. A coywolf."

"So not as dangerous?"

"More dangerous. Gladys, keep a close eye on the children from now on."

Paul sits down. "What do you mean, more dangerous?"

"They're shapeshifters. Attracted to our—our excesses. They have the skills of a coyote *and* a wolf. But they don't fear us like coyotes do, and they don't respect us like wolves do."

The African women slip back into their chairs, but there's an eerie silence, like they've seen a werewolf. Paul watches them, watches the children, shakes his head.

"You know, they are so afraid. Always so afraid."

"But why? We just have to be a little more careful, that's all. We have to get rid of the bunnies."

"I try to tell them. You are in Canada. They cannot hurt you."

"The coywolves? You mean the coywolves can't hurt them?"

He studies me for a moment. "When I was in Pakistan, I got kidney problem. Doctor gave me three months to live."

"Wow. What happened?"

"I had a friend who was a follower of Yeshua. He said: *Come to my church, and we will pray for you.* I knew what that meant—a Muslim going to church. But I was desperate. I did not tell my family. I told them I was going to library. I went three times to the church. Three Sundays in a row. The pastor put his hand on my—right here." He places his hand on his stomach. "And he prayed. After the third time, I went back to doctor. He said I was healed—the disease was gone! He said it was a miracle. After that, I wanted to know this Yeshua. I went to the church many times, and then my family found out. The pastor said: *You must leave Pakistan. They put a ransom on your head. They will kill you.* Before I left, he gave me a new name. Paul."

Gladys is listening intently.

"It is beautiful," Paul says. "It is more beautiful than—I have nothing to fear." He motions to the Africans. "But they cannot forget the killing. They are still afraid."

"But why? Why are they afraid? They are in Canada now."

"Their families are dead because they were Christian. Just like in Pakistan. Sikhs and Christians. Nominal Muslims. Shia. All of them persecuted, even killed sometimes. You think those persecutors are all over *there*? Cannot touch you here?"

"I ... I don't know. I try not to think about it, I guess. Why aren't you afraid?"

He presses his fist against his chest. "I have God inside."

For some reason, I think of my father, sitting in church in his crumpled suit. Upright pews and Father, illiterate, thumbing through the old hymnals, touching the pages, and the sacred words touching him back. Then at home again, and the deep shame of not being able to read the cereal box or the newspaper or the advertisements on the bus stop bench, of being shut off from the sanctions and discourses of society, shut off like one of Foucault's madmen. And the deep shame of always pretending, shrouded in a conspiracy of silence. And he so utterly defined himself by what he was not—by what was missing. And the shame I felt as a child, of having a father who couldn't read, couldn't help me with my homework—determined not to be like him, not to let others be like him—until later, later as an adult, his pain became my own, somehow, and finally I understood. I understood the need for isolation, the need to be invisible, to roam around in the silence of my mind where things are hidden like grizzlies tucked into snowy caves.

Charlie comes out, carrying the ant farm. He limps over to the far corner of the garden, drops the ant farm in the dirt, takes the cover off.

I walk over. "What the hell are you doing?"

"Gotta get rid of these ants."

"But they're Jed's."

"Big, big problem if these ants get out in The Booth."

He takes a soup spoon from his back pocket and begins to scoop out the dirt. I'm dumbfounded, but I say nothing. As their tunnels and caves collapse, the ants become manic, scurrying up and down Charlie's arms and careening through the dirt in a frenzy. And then the strangest thing happens. Red ants begin to appear out of nowhere—a dense swarm of them. I look closely, and Charlie looks, too. Scores of red ants are rushing in like a Roman army unrolling from every side, launching attacks against the black ants. Several pairs of ants rear up in battles for dominance— which at first, it seems, is attained by physical size. A black ant stands on a tiny clump of earth and decapitates its rival, but then several red ants instantly swarm around it in a shapeless affront, striking from every side.

Then I notice something truly astonishing: The red army, it appears, is strategically coordinated. There is a front line comprised of smaller ants— the weak, the elderly, and the disabled, perhaps—masses of disposable troops sabotaging the boundaries of the black ants. Advancing from behind come higher-calibre fighters with burly heads and torsos. Yet despite its strategic structure, the red army has no centre, no boundaries. It's a swarm: Power and communication do not appear to flow from a central source, but from—perhaps—polycentric modes of command, with every component communicating, somehow, with the others in a throng of distributed networks, ubiquitous and fleeting all at once, throwing the black ants into a state of consummate paranoia, and operating much like a terrorist network. I'm appalled as I watch—and relieved that the children aren't around: They have spent hours admiring the engineering feats of the black ants under Jed's tutelage.

I think of Anwar al-Awlaki: American citizen exterminated by his own government for acts of terror. A product of home-grown terrorism, immune to traditional military machines that operate like a chess board with its pieces—the king, buffeted by his officers, kept within the headquarters of his own domain, secure and distant from the front lines and issuing commands across a finite number of black-and-white checkered squares. A traditional army is merely shadow boxing in the presence of home-grown terror. You cannot hunt down a swarm, an enemy that is virtual; military might in this scenario is impotent—if you strike the head, another one surfaces. The response? You create a police state. You dominate your subjects, assassinate rebels, and carry out mass arrests. But dominance is always resisted, and control is always finite. So you learn to operate like the enemy: You become a network. You step over the threshold and into the unseen.

Olga comes into the garden, lights up one of her slim cigarettes.

"Charlie!" she says. "What are you doing?"

He holds up the empty ant farm. "Ants gone."

"Good. Throw container in dumpster."

Olga presses the cigarette between her lips. "Thin cigarettes. Smoke less."

"You smoke twice as many of them," Paul says. "Watch," he says to me. "She will have two instead of one."

"Yes, yes," Olga says. "But skinny cigarettes make me *feel* like I smoking less." She snorts, then turns her attention to me.

"You trying to save Jed's ants?"

"Well ... it's kind of cruel, don't you think?"

"You miss him?"

"What? What makes you think that?"

"Where you get that earring?"

My hand moves instinctively to my ear; I press the earring between my fingertips.

"Ha, ha, yes. You like him? Yes, yes. You do. You know what?" She raises her voice. "He's *gone!* Not coming back. Find another man, Sarah. Nice man. At The Booth. Nice African man, right Gladys?" She lifts her chin toward Gladys, whinnies like a horse, and for the first time, Gladys is sullen and unresponsive.

"Jed wants me to go to Israel," I say defiantly.

"He never coming back," Olga says. "He find Jewish girl. Why he want *you*? He will forget you."

"He wants me to go to Israel," I say again to Gladys, to Paul and Esperance.

Out of the corner of my eye, I see Mohammad stationed in the door-way. How long has he been there? He's watching and listening. He wheels over. Somehow, he has understood our conversation.

"Go. You go. Jedediah good man. He love." He grips the wheels of his chair, and I can see his thick fingers on Jed's face—I can see his love for Jed and Jed's love for him. I twist the earring through my piercing.

"Jedediah," Mohammad says, pointing at the earring.

"Yes. Jed." I take it off and pass it carefully to Mohammad. He turns it in his fingers, and it turns patina green, like Quarry Lake in the morning.

Act Five: Trumpets
(YOM TERU'AH) — TISHRI (SEPTEMBER-OCTOBER)

I flop into my Lazy-boy with a bowl of Lucky Charms, picking out the marshmallows. The place is filthy. Dust and dirt everywhere. Piles of books, dead flies. The pictures on the wall are straight, though. I cannot tolerate crooked pictures. I live in the kitchen and living room mostly, sleep in my Lazy-boy a lot. All the doors in the hallway and the basement are shut. I cannot bring myself to clean their insides.

I've lost myself, somehow—like I woke up one day and decided— just decided—that I have no people, no attachments, no roots. Because my people, my attachments, my roots are the refugees—but the earth has shifted, caved in: They are preparing to leave The Booth—writing resumes, applying for jobs, looking for housing. They are occupied by the future; I, by the past. And yet ... and yet. I've never taken the final step that they have—that irrevocable step over the threshold of everything that is known, everything that is palpable, everything that is earnest—all of it compressed into a series of translucent vignettes, skipping across the waters. And perhaps that is what makes all the difference.

I turn on the news. There is a refugee crisis, the anchorman says: Ghettos are forming in France and Germany—internment camps. Germany has brought in swarms of refugees, because she cannot recover from her guilt, it seems—she cannot get past the doorkeeper. And so history is coming around again: tensions and squabbles and rapes and murders— and the white supremacists are rearing up, bringing Germany and Europe to their knees.

I think of Israel, the Jewish quarter of the Middle East. Set apart, surrounded by the children of Ishmael. And Ishmael's mother, Hagar, sent into the wild to weep by a spring of water, and an angel coming to her. *You will bear a son*, the angel tells her. *His hand will be against everyone, and everyone's hand will be against him.* This I know from the Old Testament stories my father taught me in my childhood. They seem to be coming true: bombs and explosions—and now random stabbings everywhere in Israel; red ants reared up against black ants. I worry about Jed. He hasn't called, hasn't emailed. I think about a story my father taught me as a child. Jesus kneeling in the dirt beside a disabled man on a mat. The man trying to get into a pool of water because the water is holy and it heals people. And Jesus looks the poor bugger in the eye, that poor bugger sitting in his filth and stench, and he asks: *Do you want to get well?* And the man says: *I can't.*

And I don't know what I would have said. If Jesus had asked me. But I wish he would ask. I wish he would just ask me. Because I'm afraid. I'm afraid that the war will come here. I'm afraid that it has already come. And then the anchorman like a prophet brings my fears into being: An explosion has gone off at The Booth.

* * *

The explosion went off in the kitchen, excavating it like the quarry. Gas leak, is the story. Paul has been let go. I'm standing among the refuse, frozen. There's no blood anywhere. That's a good sign. Olga comes in, stands beside me.

"African families gone. Moved out. Too afraid."

"But why?" I ask her. "What happened? Was anyone hurt?"

"Hurt? Of course they hurt! They *all* hurt. They come to Canada for peace. Not—not—Oh my God. Oh my God! What we do now? That Gladys! Stupid woman! Never study! Always in kitchen eating. She went to toilet. Left Amos in kitchen, then explosion happened! Stupid, stupid, *stupid* girl!"

"What? What are you saying? Amos?"

"Yesterday, chasing bunnies. Today, *dead!*"

The air is thick, as though angels are brooding over us, as though we're standing in a gas chamber. There's no smell. Nothing. Just blackness like the coal mines. In the corner is a remnant of the piano that Don de Dieu liked to play, and on top of it is Jed's trumpet, still golden, with bits of light winking in its keys; it survived the blazing furnace like the Jews of Babylon.

"Where are Mohammad and Haya?" I ask Olga.

"In their room."

"Are they moving out?"

"They staying here until we find another place for them. We bring food from restaurant. Big problem!"

I slip out of the kitchen before Olga erupts into one of her rants, find Mohammad and Haya's room, knock on the door. Haya answers, and

I kiss her three times and hold onto her, hold on tight. We weep in the doorway, and my tears soak into her hijab. Mohammad wheels up and bows his head like an Istanbul crocus, a *colchicum*: the emblem of life inside severity, life inside harsh mountain winds.

"Come," he says after a few moments. "Come and sit." There are no chairs, only a vibrant red-and-green carpet and a plant with red blossoms and sharp thorns. Jed's Crown of Thorns.

"From Jed," Mohammad says. He picks it up to move it out of the way, but a thorn pricks his finger, draws blood. "Ach!" he exclaims, dropping the plant on the carpet and spilling its dirt.

Haya gets some paper towels.

"Let me help." We kneel down, mop up the dirt, and Haya wipes the blood from Mohammad's finger.

"Stop," Mohammad says. "Stop!" He brushes her away.

"Mohammad, what happened? What happened in the kitchen?" I lick my lips, taste the salt.

"Amos! Died!" He begins to speak in rapid Arabic, then moves back into English.

"They say someone left gas on in kitchen. Don't believe. Don't believe! Bomb! Like bomb in my taxi in Syria. Same."

"But … but how do you know this?"

"Hussein and Fatima. And their family. All their friends coming here at night. Now? All gone. All."

"What?"

"Gone. After explosion."

"That doesn't prove anything."

"Sarah, I know. I *know*. Why we come here? Get away from bombs!"

"But the police. Did they do an investigation? What did they say?"

"They say gas. But the boy, Sarah. The little boy, Amos! Killed!" He folds over and begins to sob, wrenching like an osprey calling for its young, and Haya sits quietly on the floor, looking at the blood on his fingers.

There is a light tap on the door, and some of the other students come in: Ahmed, Mayada, Hamid, Fedva, Sadya, and a few children. They crowd into that tiny room and stand around Mohammad as he weeps in his chair, and I stand with them. I want to put my hand on Mohammad. I want to comfort him, but I can't. I know that. I can't touch a Muslim man. And my heart aches because I want so much. I want so much to be yoked into

Mohammad's pain. And then Mohammad takes my hand and he takes Haya's hand and he clutches us tightly, and I am astonished. And then we all crowd into Mohammad; we crowd in like the stone table and chairs at the Sparrowhawk tarns.

* * *

At home, the answering machine is blinking. I know it is Jed. I know like the knowing that happens before thunder strikes, the waiting—the waiting, wide-awake with quick breaths. I press the play button. His voice is faint, far off like a wild place, but close, too, like wind in the woods.

"Sar-ah, I miss you … I miss you! Autumn is so lovely here. The heat of summer is past; the rains are over. Olives are ripe—and so many birds. It's lovely and warm. I want to hear your voice … " Then there is crackling, and he's gone.

I listen to his message again and again, then dial his number. I don't know what time it is in Israel. The phone rings several times, and then I hear his voice.

"Yes, hello?" There is an echo after he speaks, like he is in a big, hollow room.

"Jed! It's Sarah. Jed, there was an explosion at The Booth. The Africans, Jed. Gladys and Amos. Amos—he died!"

Silence. He says nothing.

"Jed? Are you there? Jed?"

"Little Amos? Gladys' little Amos? What happened?"

"I can't believe it, Jed. I just can't believe it. They were in the kitchen. Gladys and Amos. Gladys went to the toilet, and then the kitchen exploded."

"What happened, Sarah? What *happened*?"

"Someone left the gas on in the kitchen. But Mohammad? He thinks it was a bomb. He thinks it was Fatima and Hussein's friends. They've been coming at night."

"What did the police say?"

"They investigated. They said it was gas. Someone left the gas on. Paul, the cook, was fired."

"I'll come back, Sarah."

I am overcome by emotion. He is everything right now. He is everything I need. His strong, gentle presence. I need it. We all need it—we need *him*. I begin to sob.

"Sarah, wait for me. Things—things are intensifying here. Knife attacks, bombs. It will be difficult to leave the country—to … to leave my father. I won't be able to contact you regularly. But I will come. I promise you, I will come. Sarah? Why don't you come here? Just for a while. To get away."

"I … I don't know. I don't think I can leave just now. I don't think I can leave the families, you know?"

"Of course. But—in case you change your mind, I'll send you a contact—just outside of Jerusalem. A guesthouse. In case you—in case you want some space. If you come."

* * *

I'm at home. There's a knock at the door. No one comes here. I answer, and two police officers greet me.

"Hello … Sarah? Could we have a few moments of your time?"

"What for?"

"You work at the refugee home, don't you? The Booth?"

"Yes."

"We want to ask you a few questions."

"Okay." I don't think to ask them in, so they stand outside on the deck. The shorter one is muscled up and doesn't appear to have a neck. The other one is older with a flat white face and thin lips.

"What type of work do you do at The Booth?" the white man asks.

"I teach English."

"Ever noticed any strange behaviour from your students? Ever noticed any aggression? Any threats?"

"Like what?"

He licks his lips, deposits bits of spittle in the corners of his mouth.

"Like anything," his partner says. "Ever seen anything out of the ordinary?" He has a clipboard and a pen, ready to discharge.

"Not really." And then all at once I remember Hussein. The subtle hints: radical Islamic teaching, hatred of the West. But would he be capable of carrying out such a plan? I say nothing.

"Okay. Where were you when the … when the explosion went off?"

I think back. "I was here."

"Can anyone verify that?"

"No. I was alone. What happened? Was it a bomb?"

"Miss, we don't know anything right now. Just checking a few things out. That's all."

"Sometimes visitors came at night. Intimidated people."

"What kind of visitors? Where did they come from?"

"From the east side of the river. That's all I know—I was never there to see what was going on."

He shakes his head and writes down a few notes in neat, block letters. "Thank you for your time, Miss."

I watch as they leave, keep watching after they're gone, and suddenly I find myself resenting them, resenting their stiff uniforms and their aloofness and their presumption. They know nothing. They know nothing of the things I know. They are mediocre men going about their little lives in a shell of self-importance.

Wild geese fly low in the moonlight, not in v-formation but in a straight line, like a thin thread being pulled across the horizon, and the constellations are booming all around. I make myself some warm milk, sink into my Lazy-boy with a Hudson's Bay blanket.

Fatima and Hussein. Are they killers? Terrorists?

And then it comes to me, slowly.

The terrifying thought comes to me—the thought that there is within me a small particle that is entangled with them. The vague impression that their depravity is something that I—I, so removed from their way of life—can comprehend. Or maybe even something that—something that is in me—but no. No, they are—no. They are animals. If they are terrorists, they are animals. But this singular thought, this impression, terrifies me. What if I am *like* them? What if—what if I *am* them—like Catherine is Heathcliff?

And I know that I have to go to Israel. I *have* to go. I have to find out who I am. And who Jed is.

Act Six: Atonement

I'm on a plane headed to Frankfurt, then Tel Aviv. Olga has given me two weeks. Am I crazy? I have nothing but an address to a guesthouse outside of Jerusalem. And Jed's phone number. He's expecting me, I hope. I phoned, left a message. Maybe I shouldn't have abandoned my students. But the pain. The pain, washing over them like waves being pulled across Quarry Lake in a high wind, is more than I can bear.

It's night; there's coal-blackness outside the airplane window when we land. No one to receive me. I rehearse what I will say to customs—Mohammad and Haya have prepped me.

"It's the Middle East. They want to know why you travelling alone. Why woman travelling alone. Say you visiting friends. Touring country."

True, partially—but I'm *escaping* to the Middle East, just as its people are escaping to the West. I move into the customs lineup, nervous—nauseous. A female officer beckons me. What can she do to me, really? I haven't done anything wrong. I'm not a criminal. She looks at me briefly.

"What is the purpose of your visit?"

"I'm on vacation."

She stamps my passport and passes it back to me. That's it? I wait for my luggage, then go outside and board a sherut that is headed for Jerusalem. The sherut won't leave until it's full. We need six more people. A tall woman with grey, wiry hair pushes her way on board. There are two empty seats across the aisle, but she moves my bag over, takes the seat next to me, and begins speaking rapidly to the driver. In Hebrew, I presume. He responds with a few sharp yelps, gesticulating wildly. They seem to be arguing about whether or not the sherut is full enough to leave.

"Two more," he says, waving two of his fingers. "Two more!" She shakes her head and mutters something under her breath. In Hebrew? Yiddish? Arabic? I can't tell. But her accent sounds French. Finally, the driver takes his seat and pulls the sherut away from the airport.

"Are you here on vacation?" I ask the woman, a bit meekly.

"No. I live here six months of the year. The other six in France."

"Oh. What type of work do you do?"

"I'm a professor. And a writer. I'm writing a book on the catastrophe in Europe. It's going to erupt. France? It's going to erupt if we don't do something. Germany? Too late. Well, it's too late for France, also. No-go zones—like military camps; they follow their own rules. But no one believes it's happening. And I teach a philosophy course here at the university each fall. What about you?"

How do I answer? I give her my rehearsed reply. "I'm visiting friends. Touring the country."

We chat intermittently, and I look out the window, see streetlights fuse with the faces in the glass. After a few stops, the sherut pulls up to an empty, sloped street. It's dark. The driver stands and points at the street.

"There," he says to me.

"Where? Where is the guesthouse?" I'm holding a small scrap of paper with the address scrawled on it.

He points at the street sign. "There."

"But where is the house?"

The driver and the professor erupt into a heated exchange, flinging words at one another.

"Let me see your address," she says, snatching the paper from my hands.

"This isn't it," she says to the driver. "This isn't it!"

"Yes, yes, yes!" he responds.

Finally, she relents. But she looks dubious. "Go ahead," she says to me. "It was nice to meet you."

"Good bye." I step out of the sherut and go around to the back of the vehicle for my luggage. The driver opens the hatch but makes no move to assist me. I haul my bag out of the trunk and let it slam backside-up on the pavement, then flip it over onto its wheels.

"Will you wait here for a few moments? In case it's the wrong street?"

"No."

"Oh. Okay." I will have to rely on the famed Middle Eastern hospitality, I think, if I'm in the wrong place. I'm not afraid, exactly. Just wary. The hill is steep, and it winds down to a cluster of brown villas. I walk up to one, ring the bell, and an elderly gentleman opens the door.

"Hello, welcome. You are welcome. Come in."

I show him the address. "I'm looking for the Bethel Guesthouse."

"Down the hill," he says, scowling, and closes the door.

I walk a little further, come to a set of stairs. The moon is just ahead, almost at eye level, filling the sky like a great golden shekel, and within its contours I see a lemon tree, an olive tree, and rose bushes. I knock on the door. An elderly woman with tight red curls and pencilled eyebrows answers.

"Sarah?"

"Yes."

"Come in. I'm Esther."

The house is large and packed like an osprey nest. There's a menorah on almost every table, piles of folded laundry, glass jars and vases, baskets of artificial flowers, a bowl of glass pomegranates, three televisions, books and newspapers, suitcases, a guitar, a tambourine, a piano, and a rolled up Israeli flag in the corner. A skin of dust is spread over everything. The kitchen table, long like a casket, is set with plastic plates and cutlery and lovely blue water glasses with golden rims.

"One night?" Esther asks. "You're staying one night?"

"I think so. What about you? How long are you staying?"

She chuckles. "I've been here thirty years. You're from Canada? Me, too. Ontario. Brampton."

"Why are you here? Why did you move here?"

"My husband is a sabra—native-born Israeli, fifth generation. No way *he's* leaving. So I came here when we were dating, made aliya. Later, we got married. Do you know what aliya is? It's IDF service—the Israeli Defense Force—if you want to live in the Land, you have to do it. I'm part Jewish, you see. Jewish grandmother."

"Oh. Do you like it here? Do you like operating the guesthouse?"

"It pays the rent. And we like to teach the guests. We teach them about the feasts."

"Like Passover?"

"Yes. Like Passover. You look tired, dear. Let me show you to your room." She leads me down a series of short hallways and several sets of stairs with large landings. After we descend into what feels like the catacombs of the building, she brings me into a tiny room with thick white walls and a narrow bed.

"Forgive me. It's the bomb shelter. It's all I have right now. Breakfast is between eight and ten. Goodnight, dear."

Just before she shuts the door, I hear jackals carolling, their song float-ing above the earth like a spray of mist. I sit on the corner of the bed and marvel that I am here, here in the Holy Land.

* * *

I get up at seven. Phone Jed. No answer. The dining room is empty, except Esther, who is seated at the head of the table reading a newspaper.

"You're up early, dear," she says. "Help yourself to the fridge. I haven't put out breakfast yet."

The fridge is stuffed like a jar of olives. I take out some bread and jam, bring it to the table. A large man in cat pyjamas and slippers comes into the room.

"Good morning," he says to me. "You're the new girl. Are you American?"

"Excuse me? No, I'm certainly not. I'm Canadian. Don't confuse the two."

He smiles. "Okay, sweetheart. And I'm Irish. Don't confuse me with an Englishman."

"Deal. Will you join me for some bread and jam?"

Esther raises a pencilled eyebrow. "Don't try that with a Middle East-ern man. He'll think you're a loose woman—or worse."

"That's ridiculous. I talk to Middle Eastern men all the time."

"You talk to Middle Eastern men in Canada. You don't talk to Middle Eastern men in the Middle East."

Cat man and I sit down together. He's a big man, and his pyjama buttons pull away from their button-hole girdles. The dining room begins to fill: Catherine from Tahiti, Merv and Mary from Iowa, Peter and Tabitha from New Zealand, Jenny from Toronto. Jenny is Chinese, but she has mocha skin—as though a great grandfather from northern India or Afghanistan mixed himself into the lineage like a Bloody Mary. She walks with a limp.

"Blisters," she says. "And swollen ankles."

After breakfast, she offers to take me for a walk on the road to Emmaus, which is a few kilometres from the guesthouse. It's a dirt road, yellowish, and steeped in story: After Jesus was crucified, two of his friends were walking on this road, and Jesus appeared and walked with them for a while. But they didn't recognize him; they couldn't see the Messiah in their midst.

"Has that ever happened to you?" Jenny asks. "Like, something significant was right there, and you couldn't see it? Watch out for diamond-head vipers. They're deadly. Are you going to Jerusalem today? I'll go with you. Show you around."

I'm grateful—until later, when I see what she's wearing: a pink sunhat the size of a fruit platter with a string pulled tight beneath her chin. I suppress a chuckle.

"Keeps the sun off my face." She looks at my naked head. "Make sure you bring plenty of water. People have died here of dehydration."

Jenny and I spend the morning together. She tells me about the State of Israel, how it was birthed in a single day, May 14, 1948, when the siege of Jerusalem was broken in the War of Independence and a state was born—the promise of HaShem becoming a reality: *In a single day, I will make you a nation.* She talks about the kibbutzim, collective farming communities that were pivotal in establishing the new state.

"You can stay in one of them, you know; Kibbutz Gesher is a good one. It's on the Jordan River. There's three bridges there—you know, *gesher*—it means bridge. You can see the Jordanian hills from the bridge. Lots of German Jews started kibbutzim, you know."

She shows me where the bus stops are, how to pay, where to get off. There is English on the signs, but it's small, couched between Hebrew and Arabic, difficult to read. She takes me to the Old City, the original Jerusalem, walled and exquisite. This is where I will meet Jed, I hope. Jenny advises me to leave another message on his phone, tell him I'll wait for him at a place called Christchurch Guesthouse.

We wind through narrow, stone streets upholstered with mounds of fruits and vegetables and meats and spices: sulphur yellows, burnt reds, and nut-browns shaped into pyramids. Tiny roadways jut out erratically into cloisters of living quarters compressed into crooked boxes. People rub into one another, and the tourists wear calf-length polyesters and khaki shoulder bags strapped tightly across their chests. The *otherness* of it all is stifling. We come into the Muslim quarter near Damascus Gate, where a German girl and a police officer were stabbed a week ago. Layers of dust and heat wrap around each other, and black hijabs descend on the corridors like thunder clouds. Jenny begins to walk briskly.

"Walk close to the edge. Keep your purse on the outside. If you get stabbed, your bag will protect you."

She's paranoid. I push through the middle of the road, pressed in on both sides by merchants and their chattels, keeping an eye on Jenny's pink bonnet as it bobs through the throng of people. At last, we reach Christchurch. A violinist is there with a Spartan bicycle and a sound system in a makeshift wagon. She lays out a small tattered carpet in front of the bike.

"I'll leave you here," Jenny says. "Call us at the guesthouse if you run into trouble. And if you take a taxi, make sure it's a Jewish driver. Do *not* get into a cab with an Arab." She kisses me briefly on the cheek and steps into the deluge of people.

The violinist picks up her instrument. She wears an orthodox scarf wound up high like a turban. She has three or four sweaters on and a long shapeless skirt and high socks and no shoes because she's standing on her carpet. Not an inch of her skin is visible: only her face and her hands, lovely in their coarse candour. She begins to play. The people stand in the music, and their thoughts and motions become slow and laboured like a climber's breath at high altitudes. She jerks back and forth at the hips like an Israeli at the wailing wall and pushes her bow fitfully, her elbow high. There is nothing graceful or delicate or lovely about the currents of her music: It is fierce and it is terrifying, because it is bringing something into being, something that didn't exist before.

I close my eyes and allow the utterances to pass over my body, through my intellect, and into my spirit. And then I feel a beard in the crowd of Jewish and Arab men—and eyes like the coal mines. I open my eyes and he is there, beside me, watching me. And the spirit of the violin is moving through him like it's moving through me and through the crowd, because the violin has a consciousness of its own: The bow and the string touch each other, and all of their knowing, all of their volition and purpose, all of their appetites stiffen in the air like cream whipped into high peaks.

"You're here," Jed says when the violinist takes a break to talk with the people. He's wearing a wrinkled button-down and Birkenstocks. "I can't quite believe it. It's good to see you, Sar-ah. Are you hungry? Thirsty?"

"Of course I am. I've been wandering around in the heat all day. It's hot. Too hot."

"This is the nicest time of year. Let's get you something to eat." He takes my hand and pulls me out of the Old City and through a maze of yellow-dirt streets that converge on a large courtyard.

"This is it," he says. "This is the refugee home. We call it House of Refuge."

"What? This is it? But where are the guests? Where are the rooms?"

"Here. Right here. The House of Refuge is shaped like the Hebrew letter B, or *beth*, the first letter of the word *bayit*, which means *house*."

"Oh. What does a Hebrew B look like?"

He stoops down and draws a square in the dust. "Well, the proto-Sinaitic inscriptions depict a simple square ... "

"Proto-*what*? Can't you speak English?"

"Okay. Well, let's see. Well, the inscriptions are part of an alphabet that was used to record the Semitic dialect that the miners spoke."

"You mean like the coal miners—the quarry!"

"No—no, not really. They mined turquoise in Serabit el Khadim. And Hebrew is similar to that—to their dialect. So the archaeologists were able to decipher the alphabet. So. The proto-Sinaitic inscriptions depict a square. Then a dot is added, possibly to indicate a fire burning in a hearth."

He puts a dot in the square. "That dot is our courtyard—where you are now standing. The place of coming together. Then, later, the square opens, and we have a door."

He draws several versions of squares with openings and lines moving inward and demonstrates how the square becomes a matrix and the matrix rotates into a *beth*, a Hebrew B with an opening—an opening to the stranger who comes looking for shelter. He goes on. He describes the conversion of proto-Sinaitic to proto-Hebraic.

"The giving of the Torah to Moses on Mount Sinai—you know, the Ten Commandments—*Thou shalt have no other gods before Me. Thou shalt not make unto thee any graven image, or any likeness of anything that is in the heavens above.* Do you know them?"

"Of course I do. I didn't grow up in a cave. My father taught me. *Don't steal. Don't lie. Don't kill.* That kind of thing."

"Okay—so the Semites, who wrote their language in pictographs, transformed the images from hieroglyphics to consonants because of the second commandment: *Do not create images of anything in the Heavens.* So from pictograms—drawings that imitate events and objects, concrete reality—they created ideograms, using signs to represent abstract ideas—and then phonograms, where the sign represents not images but sounds—and eventually modern alphabets with abstract characters were born."

We are standing in a walled courtyard. The heat of the sun is bearing down on us and the sound of his voice carries the ripples of the quarry and the groans of the woods and the echoes of words spoken from beyond what to me is comprehensible.

I look at his drawings, and after a while I can see it. I can see a house in the *beth*.

"So. Each of the main walls in the House of Refuge, the *beth*, has a place for community—a kitchen, a chapel, a sitting room, bathrooms."

"Community bathrooms?"

"Let's get something to eat. Get out of the sun."

"Good idea."

We cross the courtyard and enter a large dining area, and the contrast with the hot and quiet sun is like another wall, at first. The room is alive with people and conversations and folk music and kitchen sounds—banging pots, running water, shouts and whistles, and the occasional smashed dish with its attendant expletive. There is a long table with food, buffet style—salads, olives, cold meats, and at the far end, cakes—and a dozen small tables with green, red, and blue tablecloths. We fill up two plates and sit down. Jed knows everyone, of course, and while I eat, he greets people, hugs them and kisses them. I watch the colours and lines of his face and beard fusing with other lines, other colours, fusing with them and forming new horizons. He enters into small conversations, and he's quiet—but present, as though each word, no matter how trivial, anticipates a greater whole.

Finally, we're alone at our table, and his hands come to rest on the violent red cloth.

"Do you want to talk, Sarah? About the explosion?"

"I don't know."

We're silent.

"I just—I don't know. I don't understand what happened. And I'm not sure I want to be there anymore—at The Booth. It's just—it feels like I'm in over my head. I don't know what—I don't understand these people. And I don't know how to teach them. I mean, how many times do I have to tell them that you can't mix tenses? Or that a *he* is not a *she*? There's rules, you know? Like rules in a game—Monopoly. Or chess. You have to follow the rules, or the game doesn't work. And it's just—it's simple things. Over and over I tell them, and they keep making the same mistakes. Why aren't they learning? Is it me? Is it my teaching?"

"Maybe you're asking the wrong questions. Maybe you're trying to take something apart that doesn't exist unless it's together."

"Go on. But be brief, I beg you."

"Do you remember that Persian carpet in my old office?"

"Well, yeah."

"It dates back to the nineteenth century. It has the mark of a festival, don't you think? The colours, and the stems and blossoms—they bring to presence another reality. Something repeated. The entire Middle East is crowded into that tiny office!"

"It's a carpet, Jed. It matches the paint."

"Okay. Then why not replace it with something new, an imitation for a few hundred dollars?"

"Seriously? That carpet is a work of art. The Iranians regard carpet weaving as the most elevated art form achieved by man!"

"Exactly! That carpet is part of a *body* of work. It's part of an unfinished event, because the art of carpet weaving is still in the making—it's still unfolding. Maybe you need to think of your students the same way. Maybe you're trying to force something into being, like—like getting a product ready for market."

"I don't know what you're talking about. All I know is that some of them know the rules of grammar better than I do—but they can't apply them."

"Why are you suddenly so concerned about grammar?"

"Because you can't learn English unless you know the rules."

"Granted. But it sounds like you're taking a positivist approach to language learning. Trying to standardize and regulate—"

"—Of course I am! Because of Olga! I have to do exactly what she says. Who hired her, anyway? You?"

"Look, Sarah, you know the German scholars—and no, I didn't hire her. You know the German philosophers. You must know a little of their teachings. Have you heard of the word *Erlebnis*? What about *Erfahrung*? I can't recall the name of the philosopher who coined those words—well, he didn't coin them, of course. He just made them household words. Do you know who I'm talking about? I can't remember right now. The sun. It gets to me sometimes."

"Do you have a point?"

He pauses for several moments, his brows twitching, moving to the beat of his erratic thoughts, I think.

"Well, *Erlebnis* is something you *have*; *Erfahrung* is something you undergo. You want to understand your students?"

"Yeah, I do."

"It's not just about grammar, agreed? It's about human beings. It's about Gladys and Amos."

Little Amos. Hair shaved close to his scalp, serious little face and probing eyes. I can't bear it, to think of him. And Gladys. So exuberant and so *exacting*, all at the same time.

"You have to undergo the learning *with* your students; you can't stand outside the lines. You—well, in *Erfahrung*, people are overcome by an event, or a series of events, so that the impression never leaves them. That's when real learning happens. And I think—I think because of the explosion—"

"—I don't really want to talk about that."

"Okay. Well."

We're quiet for a few moments, and the dining room is pulsating, pressurizing when new people come in and decompressing when they leave.

"Would you like to talk about the Eritrean asylum seekers?" he asks.

"Who are *they*?"

"They're the people who are living here at the House of Refuge."

"Yeah, I would prefer that. I don't want to think about The Booth right now."

"Okay. Well. There are three families with us at the moment. A large group of them escaped from Eritrea and travelled together for some time, but they were captured in Sudan and taken to Bedouin smugglers in Sinai, who held them captive until their families could pay a ransom. But when the ransoms were paid, some of the people weren't given back to their families; they were traded—they were *traded*—they were traded like, like cattle to new captors who demanded more money. And if the families couldn't pay another ransom, the hostages were killed. The Eritreans who live here are a few of those who made it through."

He looks away for a moment, purses his lips and wrinkles up his nose, and his face in the shadows of his beard looks like a small sinkhole.

"How were they treated once they got here?" I already know the answer. I've witnessed the undertones and shortages of a nation detached, and the agony of learning how to live again after everything has been taken away.

"There's always that fear, I think—that fear of the *other*. It's everywhere. So, some of them have been jailed or interned, accused of infiltration. Their needs are staggering, as you can imagine—you've seen it in Canada. We're trying to make changes at the House of Refuge, if just for a few families. And—well, Sarah, they want to improve their English, some of them."

"Why? They're in Israel."

"The younger ones want to learn, not the older ones. English is an international language—it opens doors; they know that. I'd like you to teach them, Sar-ah."

"Where would I begin? I mean, working with people coming out of torture and imprisonment—and probably sexual servitude? How do I deal with that? This isn't even my country. I don't know what's expected of me here. At least in Canada, I'm teaching Canadian ways."

"You'll learn as you go, I guess. We all do—somehow, we have to step back into a wider field of vision. The West is fixated on personal growth, self-validation. Consumerism. These things are meaningless to the Eritreans—their thoughts are focused on not getting deported, not going to prison. Getting refugee status and staying here—or going somewhere else, finding a place that will accept them."

"But you were—when you were in Turkmenistan. You did some teaching, didn't you?"

"Yes. I trained other physicians. But, well. Sar-ah, you have something. Something students are drawn to. That's why—that's why I need you."

I feel a rattle of emotion, but I keep my mouth straight, my expression flat.

"What do you want me to do with these Eritreans?"

"I guess—as I was saying before, you have to enter into community with them. Don't try to dominate them; they are proud people. Try to create an environment—a sort of conversation, I think, in which neither you nor they remain the same."

"You're speaking in abstractions again. Rules. Give me rules. Give me strategies. Should I begin with spelling and grammar—and sentence structure? You know, get their mind off the past? Olga, the new director at The Booth, is big on that stuff. And the students seem to like it."

"Okay, well. I speak a few languages. You know that—I think you know that. And I've learned that understanding grammar is—in fact, it's innate. It's like a gene. Or a predisposition. Let me give you an example.

If I give you a list of English words, like *Israeli*, *two*, *boys*, *young*, what order would you put them in?"

I think for a moment. "Two young Israeli boys."

"Did you think about the rules before you answered?"

"What rules?"

"Rules about how to correctly order adjectives, nationality, age, and number?"

"There are *rules* about that stuff? What about other languages?"

"Every language has an operating system that is innate to its speakers. But in a lot of classrooms—well, the teacher uses conscious strategies to teach unconscious processes. But for the most part—once students have understood the scaffolding of a language, the surface-level rules—and these students learned that in grade school—well, it comes back to *Erlebnis* or *Erfahrung*, I think. It all comes back to that. Having some life together. And that, I think, can—"

"—How does a doctor know so much about teaching?"

"I suppose medicine *is* teaching. Walking with patients and learning with them. And I've discovered that our students—because of their trauma, they don't learn in the same way that they used to. So we are learning with them. And really, it's languages that I understand. I speak five of them, you know, and after a while, you start to see things."

He thinks for a few moments.

"You mentioned chess earlier. Learning how to play. Have you heard of the game Kriegsspiel? It's kind of like chess."

I nod.

"How would you teach someone to play?"

"I'd explain the rules, then I'd show him how the pieces move."

"And then?"

"And then we'd play it!"

"Wouldn't you immerse him into the world of 18th century German military schools? Wouldn't you show him maps of the French-Belgium frontier? Photos of castles, roadways, and coastlines—I mean, wouldn't you expose him to the living ancestry of the game? Learning how to play Kriegsspiel is more than a matter of learning the rules—if you want to win, that is."

"But I'm not teaching Kriegsspiel. I'm teaching English."

"Okay. How about this. We have an art therapy class here. The teacher is Hannah. They are imitating Jackson Pollock at the moment."

"Paint slinging."

"Yes! To be honest—well, I can't distinguish their paintings from Pollock's! Some students are as stiff as a Mediterranean wind, applying paint in singular, controlled flicks of the brush. Others whip the paint about in a frenzy—their smocks look like Pollock originals."

"Sounds like fun. What does it have to do with English?"

"Well. Why don't you sit in on Hannah's class? I think that will—I think then you might, after a while, begin to understand what I'm trying to say."

He's trying hard. I can see that. "Okay, Jed. I'll do that."

"I'll ask her about it. I'm sure she won't mind."

"What about your father? What is his name?"

"David."

"When can I meet him?"

"We'll eat with him tonight." His eyes roam around the room, landing on one person, then another, and then they settle on me like an osprey settles in its nest. "What about *your* father? You've never spoken about him. Or your mother."

"My mother died years ago. My father—I don't see him much."

"Why not?

"He's in a home. Dementia or Alzheimer's or something. What's the difference? He doesn't know who I am. He's angry a lot. The place he lives in, I can't go there. Too depressing. It's like a cave—a little room with no windows. Not like this place, so spread out. Are you going to show me around? Is this place like a resort?"

"The House of Refuge? It's like a compound—well, *compound* isn't the best word. Villa. It's like a villa."

"An all-inclusive resort."

"Yeah. That's it, maybe. But different. Anyway, I told you that we're a *beth*, but it's a little—it's a complicated *beth*."

"I'm not surprised."

"Each of the walls has, well, shoots, I guess you could say. Mazes with courtyards that don't seem to have any rhyme or reason until you get to know them."

"*Erlebnis* or *Erfahrung*?"

He laughs. "I'll let you decide. Before we visit my father—he's prepared a special meal for us—but before that, there's a service in the synagogue. Would you like to go?"

"Yeah, I would."

It's Friday, and the streets are quiet now, in preparation for Shabbat—the Sabbath, the holy day of rest. Every Friday afternoon, Jed tells me, people begin to transition into the day of rest; it is a day of spiritual oneness, of disengaging from the pace of the week and the frenetic preoccupation with *doing*.

"You jettison all of your weekday concerns, because you're not doing commerce, you're not doing business—no electronics, no phones, nothing. People—well, people like you, who have the weekend off—they do chores, they catch up on things they weren't able to do during the week. So they're not really relaxing; they're not really letting go of things: It's all still there and it's still churning. But Shabbat, it sort of forces you to let go; it forces you to turn to people, to relationships, to thoughts about life and who you are and why you're here. It brings you into a whole other level of being, and you're at ease in a different way. And the synagogue—well, it's a space that allows you to come in and leave the world outside."

"It sounds kind of radical. Like maybe the most radical thing you can do. Unplugging for one day of the week."

"I agree. And you know, the day seems to take on another aura," he says. "You have the sense that you're moving out of the ordinary and into a special time, a sacred, holy time. And there is—well. The service—it's a short service, and it's a lovely service. It welcomes the Sabbath and anticipates the Sabbath. So it has a lovely tone—the beauty of the Shabbat ushering in. It's a time when we have this relationship with HaShem; Israel is the groom and Shabbat is the bride. It's their time together."

"Why do you begin and end at sunset?"

He takes my hand. "Because the evening is feminine, and the morning is masculine, and the afternoon is coming together. The bride and groom coming together."

"That is so beautiful."

"It is."

We walk into the synagogue, and as we pass over the threshold I feel the aura that Jed has spoken about; all of my concerns collapse when the service begins and beautiful words like confetti are tossed into the congregation, spinning on their axes as they fall—words about creation and splendour and majesty and *joy*—great, great joy in the presence of the Jewish God that evokes in the people not laughter but awe and trembling that I can *see*—I can see them trembling like fall leaves on rooftops.

And then Hasidic melodies begin: Deep, resonant notes that travel along the smooth flooring in search of a vessel with that resolute single-mindedness that *moves* things, and each time the notes find a host, an electric current surges into the feet, then the heart, and last the mind, because it is the *feet* that compel the mind and heart; the mind and the heart left alone never cease their ruminating and philosophizing and theorizing; thus, it is the feet that the melodies seek. And then the sweet *L'cha Dodi*, welcoming the bride, and Jed is standing so close that I can feel his breath on my face.

Afterwards, we walk to David's house. He wears a long linen tunic, no shoes, and rings on his fingers. He has black horn-rimmed glasses and his teeth are stained a light caramel. I am immediately enamoured. Hannah is there, and Jed introduces me to her. She wears a veil loose around her head, but a few strands of hair have pulled free and run loose around her jawline. Her face has been cut up, a long time ago. Thin lines crisscross her cheeks and nose and forehead. She beckons us to sit at the table, long and narrow with a white cloth and blue dishes speckled in gold. There is red wine and bread braided in salt and two candles burning.

When we are seated, David stands at the head of the table and sings *Shalom Aleichem, Peace Unto You*. And peace starts to flow like a fog rolling in. Then David raises his hands and blesses us.

"May HaShem bless and protect you. May he cause his light to shine upon you and be gracious to you. May he lift up his countenance upon you and give you peace."

When he says those words, Hannah begins to weep.

"I remember my father blessing us," she says. "*May God make you to be like Sarah, Rebekah, Rachel, and Leah*. Has he, though? *Has he?*" She gets up and goes into the kitchen.

"Hannah … is Polish," Jed says to me quietly. "A Warsaw survivor. The Warsaw ghetto—her entire family rounded up like cattle—"

We hear clattering in the kitchen. "Maybe we should talk about this later," he says.

"You're the one who brought it up."

Hannah returns with a pot of soup and begins ladling it into each person's bowl. David breaks the braided bread and speaks a blessing over it. And I feel like I'm inside a Persian carpet—a cluster of symbols larger than I am, their enactment pointing not within but away to other discursive worlds.

As I watch Hannah, something changes in her expression. A grey wave moves over her face, slowly, beginning at her eyes and moving down to her neck.

Jed notices immediately and springs to his feet. "Hannah, look at me," he says sharply, moving toward her. "Hannah! Look at me."

Her eyes move to his eyes, but she is uncomprehending and begins to drift into an unknown place, an inert place. David takes the soup and ladle from her hands, and Jed holds her and steadies her, his face inches from hers.

"Hannah. Stay with me."

She looks as though she will vomit; her skin is waxy.

"Hannah."

After a few moments, her eyes come into focus and the grey recedes from her face, slowly, like waves pulling away from a shoreline.

"You're alright now, Hannah." He leads her to her chair and gives her a cup of wine.

"I'm alright, now," she says.

We are silent for several minutes.

"Hannah is our house mother," Jed says cautiously. "She watches over the women and children. And she's a landscape artist."

"Not just landscape. Portraiture, too." Her colour returns—rich cream, soft like the muddied waters of the tarns.

"How many guests are staying here?" I ask. "Are they all women?"

"They're not guests," Jed says. "They're residents."

"Are they all women?"

"There are men and women. All of them Eritrean, for now."

"D'var Torah," David says. "Word of Torah."

"My father will teach us from the Torah now," Jed says.

David begins in English, but his syntax is wild like a Stoney feral, so he moves into Hebrew, and Jed translates. David reads the story of Leah, unloved Leah, passed over for her younger sister. He teaches us about ancient pathways and their relevance to the present, and his words elevate our thoughts from trifles, from the inane, to a heightened awareness of the rhythms and meanings of life.

"I never ... I've never heard these things before," I say. "Not like this."

"The Torah is the holiest object we have," Jed says. "In our synagogue, at a special point in the service, everyone stands, and the Torah is brought out. It's taken out of a holy ark—it's been hidden, and then it's revealed—so it's new every time. And it's taken through the congregation, and people take their *tallit* and touch it, or they take their *siddur* and touch it, or they take their fingers and touch it, and they kiss it. So it's an intimate relationship we have with the Torah."

I think of the mountains, of the wild, and I think maybe it's the same thing. Because no matter how many times I hike Ha Ling, it's new every time.

* * *

Later, I'm in a taxicab seesawing up the Jerusalem-Tel Aviv highway, going home to the guest house and the bomb shelter. This road was pivotal to the War of Independence, the driver tells me. He's Arab.

"*Nakba*," he says. "Day of the Catastrophe."

He tells the story of the War, how history erected itself and stood vertical in the bloody attempt to siege Jerusalem—and Jerusalem like a father watching the hills, waiting for his sons and daughters to come home. They came, but they were clothed in the colours of war. They fought for this road, this highway, this artery—this conduit to water, food, and fuel, hemmed in like a pipeline by steep hills with delicate yellow grasses that gave terrorists camouflage and access. The terrorists set up ambushes and waited in the hills, shooting at drivers and their passengers. They put boulders on the road and waited in the trees until drivers stopped to clear the road, then swooped down on them. They waited for convoys of plated buses and trucks, clumsy and heavy with supplies, waited for them to gear down for the slow descent into Jerusalem—the cars behind them forced to decelerate—and they advanced in ranks, consuming even the stubble.

And then the response. A wild ram with knives, clubs, rifles, guns, and explosives, hammering the hills, Jews and Arabs stripped bare and left hanging, both of them.

And as he speaks, I wonder. How will I ever know anything, anything at all, about this land and these people? I look to the hills, and they're trembling in the faint light, washed in blood and singing the songs of those who died on them. The mountains in neighbouring countries are jealous of these hills, it is said. How can it be?

I get off the bus at my stop and walk down to the guest house. There's no one around, thank God. I hurry to the bomb shelter and leave the door open—the jackals are carolling. I think about Gladys and little Amos.

I think about Mohammad and Shishai and all the others. And I think about Jed, how difficult it was for him to leave them. Tomorrow, I will pack my things and move into the House of Refuge, into the *beth*.

* * *

At 9 a.m., I'm at the table with Esther and Cat man. It's a long table, but we're crowded together at one end eating bread with butter and jelly.

"Where's Jenny? And the others?" I ask.

"Sightseeing. They left hours ago," Esther says.

"Oh. That's early. A bit anal, don't you think?"

"Lots to do here."

"And you?" Cat man asks. "What's on the agenda for you today, little darling?" He's stirring sugar into his tea, and the tip of his pyjama sleeve is dipping into the cup.

"Your sleeve is getting wet."

"Oh, dear." He squeezes the edges of his sleeve with two pulpy fingers.

"I don't think I caught your name," I say.

"It's Peter," Esther says.

"Why are you in Israel?"

"Everyone has their reasons, it seems. I've been here six times. Can't stay away."

"So you're sightseeing?"

"Not this time. I'm going to Mount Carmel. There's a food bank there for Russian immigrants and Arab Israelis. I'm going to manage it. Leaving today."

"Do you speak Russian?"

"Yes, of course."

"But you're Irish. Or Scottish, or something like that."

"My parents emigrated to Ireland from Romania. They run a grocery store near Dublin. But it's getting difficult. Anti-immigration sentiments— foreigners taking all the jobs. All of that." He reaches for another piece of bread and butters it, then dips his buttery knife into the jelly, leaving little bits of butter in the jelly. "And you? Why are you here?"

"It's complicated."

Esther raises an eyebrow and begins clearing dishes. "Breakfast is over at 10," she says, going into the kitchen.

Peter looks at his watch, a black face with a purple silicone band.

"Well, my dear, I should get ready. Big day today." He pushes his chair back heavily and rambles out of the room on the soft pads of his feet.

I leave my dishes. Esther can get them—it's her job.

"Do you need a taxi, dear?" she calls.

"No. I can take the bus."

"It's Shabbat. No buses."

"Right."

"Everything shuts down on Shabbat. Most people don't go to work."

"*Everything* shuts down? Even the stores?"

"Most of them."

"That's inconvenient. How do you *function*?"

"I'll get you a taxi."

"Alright. I'll pack." I go to the bomb shelter and stuff my clothes into the suitcase, but it won't close. How did it close three days ago? I sit on it, snap it shut, and follow the narrow corridors to the back door.

"Sarah?" Esther emerges from the kitchen, tightening one of her curls with a bobby pin.

"Your taxi will be here soon." She squeezes my forearms. "All the best."

A few cats are mewing at the backdoor.

"Don't let them in the house. They're outdoor cats. Wild cats."

"But you feed them?"

"Yes. I put milk out for them. Poor things. So scrawny."

"What about jackals? Do they attract jackals?

"Don't let them in the house. I'll get the door for you." She opens it a crack, and I squeeze through with my suitcase and turn to wave, but she's moving back into the profiles of the house. I walk up the hill, breathing heavily, and a taxi is waiting. Is it mine? I don't care. I get in.

"Do you speak English?"

"Yes."

"Can you take me to the House of Refuge?" I give him the address. "It's just outside the Old City. Near Jaffa Gate."

"Yes."

The news is blaring. Israelis are addicted to news, he tells me. "We're surrounded by enemies. We have to know what's going on. All the time." We speed along the Jerusalem-Tel Aviv highway, then wind our way through busy streets and past the Old City. It is walled, of course, with thirty-four watch towers, seven main gates, and four quarters: the Jewish

Quarter, the Christian Quarter, the Armenian Quarter, and the Muslim Quarter. The driver lets me off at the House of Refuge, and I walk through the opening of the Hebrew B, into the tiny courtyard.

It's Shabbat, and it's silent.

There is no one. I look around for David's house, but it's impossible; I could never find my way through this matrix of cobblestone and flaxen walls and sky. There are tables and chairs and small potted trees in the courtyard, so I sit, walled in like a prayer pressed into the Kotel. Small homes with clotheslines fill my sightline; shirts and towels and bed sheets white and blue flapping in the breezes like impatient kites, and I think of the quarry. Mountains at night, an azure sky pinched with stars and moonlight splayed across cirrus clouds that look like an enormous rib cage, bones bleached white.

A soft voice comes in behind me.

"Hi, Sarah. Please, come." It's Hannah. She leads me into one of the courtyards extending from the *beth*. A low table braces itself against the far wall and balances several white pots alive with vines, their suction cups clinging to the wall and climbing steadily upward. Other pots, empty, huddle into the corners; their insides are painted with figures, human-like figures with hands raised up in some sort of appeal. Lining the walls are wooden frames encasing sharp shards of glass—viscous-looking glass. I don't look through it to the pale limestone behind; I look at the sharp shards and their terse denotations.

"This is the main office," Hannah says.

Inside is a counter, a sunken couch, and an antique chair that looks like a throne—tall, square back, arms with gallant curves and knobs the size of pomegranates and a cushioned seat with stiff, embroidered fabric faded and flattened by the heat.

Jed is sitting at the counter.

"Hannah, Sarah, Shabbat shalom."

"Shabbat shalom." Hannah steps aside and sweeps her hand across her body, inviting me to sit down. "I'll get tea," she says, disappearing through a rounded hobbit-like door.

Jed joins me on the couch.

"Sarah! Good to see you. I have a job for you."

"I just got here."

"True. I need you to watch the counter."

"It's Shabbat. No work, remember?"

"Hannah is teaching her art class, and it begins in a few minutes."

"But it's Shabbat."

"Well, the students still like to visit on Shabbat. No formal teaching. And they eat, of course."

"Where's the class?"

He points to the hobbit hole. "In there. Can you do it? I'll take your suitcase to your room, unpack it if you like."

"Nope. What do I have to do?"

"When the women come in, give them a name tag—" he points to a shoebox on the counter— "and bring them to the art room. And answer the phone. Oh—and maybe you could—" He looks at my face. "That's it."

"Why do they need name tags?"

"Hannah has trouble remembering names, sometimes."

Hannah returns with small cups and a thermos of tea. All the spices of the Middle East are in that thermos: cardamom and cinnamon and cloves and nutmeg—each a country of its own, dense and perplexing in aroma, emitting its own temperament and unwilling to fuse horizons with the others. Hannah pours the tea and sits on the floor across from me. I glance sideways at Jed. He doesn't offer his seat.

"Here," I say, standing. "Please sit here. On the couch."

"No, no!" Hannah says, jumping up. "No. Please. Sit."

"I will sit beside you, then." I sit on the floor, and Hannah hesitates, half sitting, half standing, like a question mark suspended in the air.

"Well, I should go," Jed says.

"Where are you going?"

"The synagogue, for the service."

"Oh. When will you be back?"

"An hour. Thanks, Sarah, for helping out."

He walks out, taking his teacup with him, and Hannah and I are left looking at the vacant couch. And I wonder if I will ever understand this man—his rhythms, the stresses and accents of his cadence. Hannah goes into the back room, and I sit behind the counter, alone. Soon a few teen-aged girls arrive; they are tall and sinewy with blue-black tattoos on their arms and hands.

"Hello. Do you speak English?"

"Yes." They gather around me, smiling shyly. One girl puts her hands on my knee.

"Are you here for Hannah?"

"Yes."

"Let me bring you." I forget the name tags. I take two hands and pull them through the hobbit hole, where Hannah is pouring tea. The room is compact and the walls are crowded with paintings and the floor tiles are indigo blue. There are long tables with benches and paper and brushes and rags and streaks of paint.

"Berry, hello," Hannah exclaims. She hesitates for a moment. "Hello Bisrat ... Yodit." She gathers them up in her arms, and I'm amazed. How is she so self-assured? With everything she has been through? I return to my post, and four middle-aged women are waiting. I bring them into the art room.

"All right," Hannah is saying, "find your seats and we'll have some sweets." On the walls are Polaroids of each student with paintings beneath them, most of them depicting black houses, black earth, black trees, black clouds. Some are of boys and girls with heads like misshapen fruit and elongated red tears or tears thinly traced like souls falling from dead bodies.

"Sarah, will you join us?"

"I have to watch the front, Jed said."

She looks at her watch. "I don't think anyone else is coming."

"But I have to answer the phone."

"You can hear it from here. Please, can you bring the name tags?"

I return to the front and wait. No more students arrive, so I decide to join the women for tea, bring the shoebox with me. They are drinking from fine china, cups and saucers paper thin, robin-egg greens and powdery pinks with silver rims.

"Sarah will do the name tags today," Hannah says.

I take a felt pen and a few name tags from the shoebox and kneel before one of the ladies.

"Can you tell me your name?"

"Shikorina."

"What? How do you spell that?"

The youngest girl, Berry, moves in. "S-h-eh-"

"I? Or E?"

"Eh."

"E?"

"You want me?"

"Yes. Please. Will you write them all down?"

"Yes." She moves to each woman and writes the name. Her letters have tails and curls and no spaces in between; they are impossible to decipher. I pour myself some tea and sit, and the women chatter in their mother tongue. Their skin is raw like umber and their eyes remind me of the coal mines with their straight, thick brows.

"Shikorina's name means sweet, like sugar," Hannah says to me. "She is precious."

"It's a difficult name to pronounce. They all are."

"Yes, but they want to keep their traditional names."

"I don't know. If I moved to a new country, I'd want a name that people could pronounce. One of my first students in Canada, Abdullah, changed his name to Ryan. So much easier. It's weird though, that he chose Ryan, because he can't pronounce the diphthong. He can't pronounce his own name."

Hannah says nothing. The women continue to chat, and there is tranquillity, and ease, and I feel like the knots inside of me are slackening.

I look at the paintings. "How do you teach, Hannah? These paintings are good—well, some of them. Do you copy the masters?"

"With the older ones, yes—kind of. But imitation really involves knowledge of essence, not reproducing other people's work, like—like an impostor. It's more like—it's like Michelangelo's nude Christ in *Crucifixion*. Do you know it? Or Mozart's inversions of *Twinkle, Twinkle, Little Star*."

"But how do you teach them without bringing up all their pain? I mean, isn't it *painful* for them to paint this stuff? In my classroom, I try to stay as far away as possible from—it helps them to forget, I think. I mean, some of these pictures—" I look at the black and grey splotches. "Some of them don't really have a lot of meaning—apart from their darkness."

"They do have meaning. You just can't see it. Or you don't *want* to see it."

* * *

Later, Jed brings me to my apartment. He leads me through limestone corridors and a small gate and motions for me to step inside. The apartment is yellowish beige with smooth walls worn down but not entirely subsumed by the decades; bumps and divots are dispersed like symbols in a cave painting.

"You said my room would be brown. And you said it would be in a house."

"This *is* a house—a spread-out house. And brown is a derivative of yellow, isn't it?"

"I'm glad you're not teaching the art class."

"You must be tired, Sarah. I'll leave you to rest. We'll have supper with my father at five, okay? I'll be back then." He squeezes my hand and leaves.

The apartment has a sitting area and three small rooms. There's a kitchen outfitted with a microwave, small fridge, wobbly table, wobbly chairs, and a wooden cart with blue plastic dishware and licorice tea bags. The bathroom has chunky green fixtures and speckled linoleum and no bath or shower—just a drain in the floor and a tap in the wall. The bedroom is just big enough for a futon and a wardrobe. I place my suitcase on the end of the futon and begin unpacking. My toiletries are in a large freezer bag, and at the bottom, in a pill bottle, is Jed's earring. I take it out and put it on my finger, turn the soft metal around and around, then put it back in the bottle, back in the freezer bag. I lie down on the futon and wait for Jed, lurching in and out of sleep.

He knocks at five, pops his head in the door.

"Are you here?" he calls.

"Yeah. Where else would I be?"

"Are you comfortable?"

"Thank you. Yes."

"Then let's go. We'll pick up Hannah along the way."

Hannah is wearing a loose golden gown, and her hair is wrapped up high in a scarf. We walk along the borders of the *beth*, and I'm getting a feel for where things are. Jed and his father live in a cul de sac that sprouts out from the dining room, across from the courtyard, across from the dot.

"We like to be close to the action," Jed says. "And the food. Tonight, you know, we're having a special ceremony. It's called *Havdalah*. It means *separation*."

When we arrive, David, Shikorina, and a young Eritrean man named Sammy are waiting.

"Shabbat shalom," David says when we enter, bowing slightly. He motions for us to sit at the dining table, and he serves warmed *cholent*, a Shabbat stew. While we eat, he tells us about Turkmenistan, and he tells us about his family members who died there. He talks about his deceased wife and about the challenges of running the House of Refuge—working with government, repairing the buildings and keeping them supplied, managing the rivalries and squabbles and disease and sickness among the residents. He laughs easily and he cries easily.

And then Shikorina and Sammy enter into the conversation. They tell about their escape from Eritrea—their capture by the Rashaida tribe in Sudan and their transfer to Bedouin smugglers in Sinai who brought them to torture camps—filthy, crowded rooms where they were shackled in metal chains and starved and beaten with sticks and burned with melted plastic and electrocuted. And of course, Shikorina was gang raped, day after day. And she's pregnant.

"I hate this baby," she says. "I will kill it." She says it without emotion.

And I feel a groundswell surging in my stomach. Hatred. Hatred for the people who did this to her—led her into the wilderness and pushed her from a cliff. *Is this Shabbat?* A holy day? A day to set things aside, separate the holy from the profane?

After the meal, David brings out a four-wick candle, a decanter of wine, and a spice box. He reads from the Torah and speaks blessings over the wine and spice box, then opens the box and passes it around. Each of us breathes in the fragrances of cloves and cinnamon and allspice and bay leaves. Then David lights the candle and holds his hands over the flame, and in the light I see his nails bruised and broken and his knobbly, wooden fingers adorned with gemstones set in silver: jasper, sapphire, emerald, topaz, and amethyst. He douses the candle with wine and we stand in the darkness—and later, we walk to the Old City and look at the stars, three of them cradled in a white ring of cloud that looks like an ermine cape and collar. And particles of the cloves and cinnamon and allspice and bay leaves drift around us and pass through the membranes of our clothing.

Afterwards, I'm folded up in my futon, and there are no jackals singing, only shouts and moans rolling around the House of Refuge like a marble on a roulette table. I open my book, *Through the Looking Glass*, and read three sentences before falling into sleep.

* * *

In the morning, Jed and I meet at Christchurch Guesthouse. He's wearing a white button down and his neck is swathed in a black scarf. It's Sunday, and the place is heaving with worshippers and tourists eating and drinking before church services and site seeing. The notes of a piano drift in from the sanctuary and wedge their way into the conversations and the frenzy, but they fail to bring about any kind of calm or candour.

Jed and I order tea and fried eggs and find a table.

"I spoke with Hannah," he says, "and she said it would be okay for you to sit in on her class—but she's finished the Pollock unit, I'm afraid. I told her about your music—the way you teach English—and, well—"

"I don't think singing will do much good in an art class."

"I don't know. I've watched your students. It's like they—well, it's like each song is an intervention, or an overture, an invitation to advance, come closer, and forget for a while. Or maybe to remember. I don't know. It's like, it reminds me of children playing dress-up—"

I raise my eyebrows.

"—they invent characters and costumes and scripts, but more important is the game itself—it has a being independent of the children's will; it commands *them* as much as they command *it*. It's like they're rehearsing for the stage. Have you ever acted on the stage? Or have you sung on a stage? I did a little of that in med school. We started an acting troupe, called ourselves *The Cure*. Didn't have much success."

"I'm surprised."

"So anyway, the rehearsals—we tend to—oh, I don't know. Partition them. We think they are somehow separated from the main event, from the live presentation. But they *are* the presentation; they're the presentation coming into being. Do you know what I mean? And I see that same thing happening in your music; the songs—well, you're not just singing little ditties, you know? Each song pulls the students in and fills them with its spirit. I think—I think that could be a balm for the Eritreans. And do you know what? They can sing, Sar-ah. They can really *sing!* They sing while they're painting, while they're walking on the road. Even their language sounds like a song."

He pauses for a few moments, fingering his beard and eyebrows.

"How long did you say you'll be staying in Jerusalem? Two weeks?"

"I'm leaving in twelve days."

"Ahh, yes. Difficult to do anything in such a short time. But that is why, Sarah—well, the way you teach is powerful. You create something with your students—something that is real. And the Eritreans, you know—well, you saw the paintings. Didn't you think the paintings had a life of their own, that they conveyed something real—something *true* that you could recognize and understand?"

I think about the bloodless tears and the black clouds.

"Don't you see? At The Booth, I always loved visiting your classroom. Your students were plucked from their hall of mirrors and yoked into something ongoing—something greater than themselves."

"By singing *Mary had a Little Lamb*?"

"Yes, by singing *Mary had a Little Lamb*. Lamb is a delicacy here in the Middle East, you know. Your songs reminded them of home."

I chuckle. "Things are different now, you know. Without you, it's not the same."

He ignores me. "You know, Hannah and her older students are painting a mural at the market today. She began the project by bringing books, pictures, and magazines to class—tactile stuff. Then they visited galleries to learn about creative techniques—you know, colour, texture, light. That sort of thing. Then they went to the surrounding community to get a living history of the place—they examined the architecture, interviewed the people, took photographs. And they did sketches of the smallest details—clothing, facial features, vegetables, fruit, stonework, stairways, arches and rooftops. Today, they begin work on the mural. Would you like to join them?"

"What are they painting?"

"Faces."

"Why do they have to sketch fruit and vegetables to learn how to paint faces?"

"Would you like to go and see? Hannah might have some food with her."

"Food? I'm all in."

The market is outside the Old City, and along the way, Jed points out shops and buildings and museums lining the loosely woven streets. We see ultraorthodox men in black robes and holy beards and *payot*; woman with long skirts and scarfs; and street signs in Hebrew, Arabic, and English. We see IDF soldiers and we see transients leaning into doorways and an ice cream shop selling five-scoop cones, each scoop in a different flavour. We see tunnels and archways and gates. And spread over all of it is a kind of loose liturgy uttered by a celestial *hazzan*.

The market is a sprawl of colour and sound and odour and movement. We step into it over an almost palpable threshold and begin our search for Hannah, up and down the narrow inlets. I repeat my question about painting portraits.

"Why do they have to sketch bananas and stairwells before they can paint a face? Seems kind of pointless."

"Not just stairwells. *Everything*. They want to be in tune with sights and sounds and memories—with the lineage of the place—before they begin. Hannah has told me—well, and I think she also wants to somehow teach this to her students—but without language, of course, because her medium is paint, of course, but she wants to show them that a painting is never autonomous; it is contextually bound. A painting—and a song, too Sarah, and maybe even a word—brings with it a *world*. So if you want to paint something, you have to really see it; you have to look *beyond* it and see it on a wider horizon—then you will understand its essence."

He walks slightly ahead, looking back at me and bumping into people as he talks, eliciting scowls and rebukes, his black scarf trailing obliviously behind. He narrowly misses a man carrying a bag of melons, but somehow the melons spill on the ground anyway and roll around like little heads. He offers profuse apologies and bends over into an inverted "L," chasing the melons and gathering them up from between feet and under tables—then drops them again. And the little heads crack open and secrete pink pulp and slender black seeds. I can no longer suppress my laughter. His white button-down is splotched in pink and he has a look of utter misery: his rescue mission has failed. The man with the melons laughs with me, and Jed straightens up and takes out his wallet to ransom the melons.

"Please, no problem," Melon Man says. "*L'shana tova tikateyvu*."

"*Shana tovah*," Jed replies. "A good year to you."

The man walks away, shaking his head.

"What were you telling me earlier, Jed? About learning how to *see*?"

He smiles and takes my hand, and we walk side-by-side.

"I don't think Hannah needs to know about this, does she?"

"I'm surprised he didn't get angry. Or at least make you pay for the melons."

"Well, it's Rosh Hashanah tomorrow," Jed says.

"The Jewish New Year?"

"Yes."

"What does that have to do with smashing melons?"

"Rosh Hashanah is the beginning of *The Days of Awe*. It's a time of introspection and repentance, and seeking reconciliation with people you have wronged. It's a time of turning to HaShem."

"Then shouldn't today be a day of absolute debauchery? Get it out of your system before you have to repent?"

"I hadn't thought of it that way."

We find Hannah and two of her students, Yodit and Bisrat, applying grey paint to the shutters of a popup market stall. We chat for a few minutes, then Hannah gives us spray cans and we begin spraying the edges of the shutters.

"I thought you were painting faces," Jed says.

"We are. This is the primer. It prepares the way for the paint, so it won't peel off. Before this, we had to sand everything down, take the rust off. Then we had to clean the surface and sand again, so the paint has something to adhere to. A lot of preparation happens before the main event."

The owner of the stall sits beside us reading a newspaper, his wares of Holy Land trinkets spread out on a table.

"Does he mind us doing this? You must have gotten permission."

"We did. The only time people will see these portraits is after the market closes, when the shutters are down and the crowds are gone."

"Then what's the point?" I ask.

"It makes a statement, I think. About the people in society who are hidden or ignored— despised even, and marginalized. That's what's happened to these girls." She looks at Yodit and Bisrat. "That's what's happened to them. Their entire identity has been rolled up into the recesses of a little metal *box*—a box of"—she looks at the owner and lowers her voice—"A box of *relics*."

After the primer dries, Jed and I work on the undercoat while the women begin their portraits on the stall beside us—another Holy Land chronicle—which they primed the day before. They draw grids, carefully measuring each square, and then with markers sketch oval heads, eyes, noses, mouths, and hair, placing each part in precisely the correct square. Hannah is exacting: She demonstrates how to use tones and shading, how to decipher light and darkness. She teaches them how to mix paint to create skin tone: Ultramarine blue, burnt umber, raw sienna, alizarin crimson, and titanium white create Eritrean skin with lips of yellow ochre and cadmium red and eyes closed behind black, curved lines like Picasso's lover in *Le Repos*. The overall appearance of the mural is geometrical: four portraits arranged into a cube. But within the cubes are the shapes and curves of a man in love with a golden muse.

We stand back to admire our work, and Hannah pulls out dates and apples from a backpack and passes them around.

"What will you paint on the stall that Jed and I are working on?" I ask her.

"Exactly the same thing."

"Why don't you mix things up, try something new?"

"With new light and thoughts and emotions, the portraits will be different. Really different. Would you like to help with the other portraits? Do the prep work? You and Jed?"

"How many murals are you doing?"

"Ten. We have to finish in time for Yom Kippur. We could use your help."

* * *

The next ten days, the *Days of Awe* from Rosh Hashanah to Yom Kippur, pass quickly. Jed and I and Hannah and the Eritreans paint the murals, and I teach them English songs while we work. And I begin to understand Jed's convictions about *being* with my students rather than holding onto static, atomistic notions—trying to isolate and define everything that is problematic with their English, deconstructing it and repairing it piece-by-piece, method-by-method. As the murals unfold, I begin to enter into genuine conversations with them—*following* conversations rather than dominating them, and the women begin to speak—real English. Not without error, of course, but without pretence. And I begin to learn. I learn about their dreams and their hardships, their former lives and their present lives. And by talking—just by talking—things come into being. Things are retrieved from the past and preserved.

And then my heart lets loose like the Stoney wild, and I talk about the explosion at The Booth. I talk about Mohammad and Gladys, Esperance and Ahmed. I talk about Amos. And then I talk about my father, the only man I've ever loved locked up in an asylum, spinning down a toilet bowl. Jed and the women listen and they say nothing. They listen. And Shikorina brings out stew with taita. The bread is porous and sour and the stew is spicy, but I eat. We eat. We roll up the meat in the taita and we eat and eat.

Shikorina says to me: "We know, Sarah. We know, we know. We know suffering, like you."

And in the early morning before Yom Kippur, we stand before our murals, each with the same subjects but with different shades of darkness, different curves and lines, different inflections, different utterances. We study them until the stall owners come and roll up the shutters and they vanish into obscurity.

* * *

Yom Kippur begins at sundown and is marked by intense prayer and five synagogue services. No cars, no buses—no food. It's the holiest day of the year in Israel, the Day of Atonement. Historically, the people confessed their sins to HaShem and to each other for twenty-four hours prior to the Day of Atonement, and then the high priest entered the Holy of Holies in the Temple to atone for the nation. As part of the atonement, two goats were selected. One was slain as a sacrifice; the other, called the scapegoat, symbolically bore the sins of Israel: It was led outside the camp, into the wilderness, and was pushed from a cliff. And then the people were clean. And when Messiah comes, he will be slain outside the camp. He will become the scapegoat and pay the ransom for his people. He will be pierced for their transgressions, crushed for their iniquities, and by his wounds, they will be healed.

Jed and I meet at nightfall in a small flea market just outside of Christchurch. There is a long table with stacks of books on it, and when I arrive, Jed is opening and closing books, holding each one like a hymnal in the palms of his hands, his black, oiled beard quivering. Lights are loosely strung above the table and a soft glow falls on the books, worn out and dusty and of little interest to anyone, it appears, except Jed, who handles each one as one would a snowflake, regarding it closely until in its evanescence it becomes imperceptible.

I walk up behind him and tap his shoulder. It's our last night together, and I've decided to wear his earring in my right ear. He turns and notices immediately, but says nothing. We stand beside the books, and I feel the hulls of doubt and discontent and ambivalence like Yom Kippur taking flight.

We walk the streets and say almost nothing as we circle the market and the Old City under the Israeli sky and the Israeli stars like a bride and groom circling under a *chuppah*. Later, he deposits me in front of my apartment and we embrace like ravens do in acrobatic flight, and he takes the earring from my ear and places it on my finger.

Act Seven: Tabernacles
(SUKKOT) — TISHRI (SEPTEMBER-OCTOBER)

It's early morning at the Quarry. The sun is rising, its light cutting across Mount Lady Macdonald, and pink-bellied clouds settle into the cups between the peaks. I'm too wired to sleep, and I can't get my mind off Jed. I wonder when he will come back for me. In a few months, he said. There's a Sudanese family coming to the House of Refuge, and he wants to get them settled. Make sure they bond with the Eritreans. I decide to visit The Booth, see what's happening.

I never enjoy driving away from the mountains; there's nothing standing before me except rows and rows of fences holding up the implacable present—an endless highway demarcated down the middle like a vein of quartz cutting through granite. As the mountains diminish in the rear-view mirror, I cross foothills and reserve land and farmlands awash in wheat and canola. All too quickly, I see the grey globs of city buildings, and it feels like I'm leaving immunity, entering a barren place difficult to navigate and holding up offerings so gaunt.

Olga doesn't greet me when I come into her office. She's scolding someone on the phone, and I take a seat in an armless metal chair.

"One moment," she snaps at the person on the line. She looks over the rim of her bifocals at me.

"Sarah. Why you here? Doesn't matter. Everyone is moved out. *Everyone*." She holds her tongue against the roof of her mouth and emphasizes the nasal "n" in a long drone of sound.

"Yazidis came yesterday. Stubborn people. Don't want to work. Leave garbage laying around. Steal supplies from storage room, even! *Just ask*, I say, *and I give it to you!* Why you have to *steal*? So—I moved out. Could not *stand* all the noise and the screaming. They scream at night, Sarah. You wouldn't *believe* it. So I moved out, my own place. New building manager in my apartment now. But the Yazidis—oh my God. They need to be busy—they need English. They need English, Sarah. Tomorrow."

"Tomorrow is Saturday. My day off." *Shabbat*, I think.

"*Tomorrow*, Sarah. You had too much time off already. The women going into panic attacks every day, sometimes every hour. We call ambulance, they bring them to hospital, give drugs, then bring them back. Oh my God. I can't take this."

She shoos me out the door and returns to her telephone conversation. I go into the dining room, and there's a woman scrubbing tables with a sponge and a bowl of water secreting the sour smell of vinegar.

"Welcome," she says, wringing her hands. "I'm Zahra." Her hair is orange, cut to the jawline, and her eyes, hazel, have the look of a wheat crop with no horizon. "I am the building manager. And I cook."

"Nice to meet you. I'm the English teacher."

"Oh yes, I have heard about you. *Sarah*. Your name is Sarah. Please, sit. Would you like tea?"

"Yes." Zahra disappears into the kitchen and I sit at a table and look around. The dining room has been renovated—grey paint with a garish feature wall and metal tables and chairs like the ones you see in an office depot sale. The wall between the dining room and kitchen—the one that Jed sealed—has been reopened like a fresh scab. Zahra brings a plate of baklava and two mugs with sliced ginger and hot water.

"Please," she says, motioning to the sweets. "Please help yourself."

I take a piece and lick the sweet, eggy nuts out of their basin. "Did you make these? They're delicious."

"Of course!" A trill of colour rinses over the high plains of her cheek bones.

"Did you know the other people here? Do you know what happened?"

"I do not know them. Olga wanted to renovate, so she moved them into duplexes on the other side of the river."

"Are they all together, at least?"

"I think they are spread out. Olga likes to separate them so they learn the culture."

I think about the Arab and African families who so recently coloured this room; their faces flood the banks of my mind, and I wonder how they are getting along. Are they finding friendship, making it through? I fear for them, for the changes I saw in them, and now, social, emotional, and linguistic isolation—minorities with no state of their own strewn over the east side. They feel like ghosts.

"Are you a refugee, too? Most of the people working here are."

"Yes. I come from Iran. I came ten years ago."

"Why did you come?"

"With the Islamic Revolution, we did not have—as women—we lost all of our rights."

"What do you mean? What happened?"

"Before, they did not make me put on the hijab. They did not tell me which music I should listen to. With the Revolution, they dictated what I should do, which dress I should wear, you know. We *had* to wear the hijab! If we did not wear the hijab, acid! Acid! They put it on your face, on your hands. Acid! And it burns your face!"

"That's difficult to comprehend."

"I had to put on long sleeves. Even in hot weather in the summer, I had to put on socks. My head had to be covered. Before the Revolution, I always wore a scarf, because I am Sunni Muslim. But you could see my hair. But that hijab, they made it tight all over our heads, our necks. I could not listen to the music I enjoyed. I could not read books. They were all censored: what you watched, what you listened to. No freedom anymore."

She speaks in low tones, as though reliving it, as though someone might hear. "Many women were fighting that regime. We posted announcements against the government, and every morning I—I was in school, and every morning, I put flyers *in* desks, *under* desks, on the walls. And when school opened, all the students were reading the flyers."

"Were you scared?"

"No. At that time I was not scared. I knew I had to fight this government; I had to fight for my rights. I wanted to do it."

She tells me about her escape with her brother, on foot at night, with wild pigs snorting at them and the border patrol making tracks in the ground with tractors, and if you walked in the tracks, they saw your footprints and came after you. And then, safe in a refugee camp, she became ill, and all of her toenails fell off.

"And now? How is it for you now?"

"I did not go into depression. I did not lose my hope."

"Are you working full-time?"

"Split shift. I come early in the morning, make breakfast and lunch and chop meat and vegetables for supper. Then I take two hours off and come back again."

"That's inconvenient."

"I do not have a choice. I need my job."

"What do you do in the two hours?"

"I am learning Arabic. So I can talk to the people." She offers me the plate of baklava. "Please, have more. Take it home with you."

* * *

The next morning, I'm in my classroom setting up chairs in a large circle, and one of my new students comes in. He wears a blue bandana around his head and tight jeans pulled down low. Large block letters are tattooed on his forearm.

"Who are you?"

"Jamal."

"Where are you from?"

"Iraq. Shingal."

"Do you speak Arabic?"

"I am Yazidi. I don't speak Arabic. You know Yazidis? You know ISIS?"

"Yes."

"You know?"

"Yes."

There are no words. We stand, we look at each other. No tears fall from his eyes. They are held in a saline catchment below the surface, a dead sea with no outlets, no access to discharge.

"Where is your family?"

"My father is gone. My mother and sisters were captured by ISIS. But they are here now. One month ago, they came. It's difficult, but we're safe. Safety."

"Are you staying at The Booth?"

"Yes."

"Do you need anything?"

"We're good."

"Have you learned any English here?"

"Yes, but difficult. You are the English teacher?"

"Yes. Your English is good."

"Thank you."

I can feel the currents of the gypsy violin building, entangling us in their field.

"Are you okay?"

"Yes. We cannot forget the past. But we must—strong. We must move forward. Do you understand?"

"Yes."

"You are the teacher. Will you teach me?"

"What do you want to learn?"

"English. I want English."

"Reading? Writing? Speaking?"

"All."

Zahra opens the door and comes in.

"Can I help you? Introduce you to the Yazidis?"

"Yes. Thank you, Zahra."

"I do not know how many will come."

"Aren't they required to come?"

"They are sick. Really sick, some of them. They have panic attacks. We bring security guards at night to watch them. Make sure they don't—how you say?—suicide. Do suicide. So they are too tired to come, sometimes."

Another Yazidi man comes in with four middle-aged women, Kodja, Dunya, Rabiya, Eli, and a younger woman, Khifshi. They are lovely; plain as hulled black lentils. The older women are quiet and shy. They sit upright in the wooden chairs, dignified as monarchs with wisps of steel grey hair showing from under their scarves and their hands folded neatly into their long, colourless skirts. The younger woman finds the recliner in a back corner, pushes it into a horizontal position, then turns away from us onto her side. The man comes over and shakes my hand. Zahra introduces us.

"This is Dakir, Jamal's brother."

Zahra says several words to him, but he doesn't respond.

"What language are you speaking?" I ask.

"Arabic. But they do not want to speak Arabic. They do speak it—well, some of them do. They just do not like to, because it is the language of ISIS. But we have no other option here; many of them do not speak English. The women do not speak English at all; Jamal and Dakir can speak a little."

I'm thankful for Jamal and Dakir.

"Okay, well, let's try a song," I say. "Hokey Pokey."

I motion for them to stand in a circle, and Jamal takes Khifshi gently by the hand and leads her from the recliner to the circle. We begin with the prepositions *in* and *out*, thrusting our hands and feet in and out of the circle. Jamal and Dakir shake their arms vigorously and kick their feet, more interested in the music and dancing than in learning English. Khifshi, however, is intent on learning, her eyes focussed on mine as she bends her mouth around the words *left*, *right*, *hand*, *foot*, *in*, and *out*.

When we arrive at the *turn yourself around* segment of the song, Dunya, one of the older women, stands rigid. She won't turn around. *What do I do?* Leave her alone, respect her wishes—but neglect her language learning and effectively isolate her from the class? I decide to take a risk. I approach Dunya, put my arms around her, and turn around with her, slowly. Will she shrink from physical touch after her ISIS ordeal? Am I doing her even more harm?

She holds me and leans into me, and in her expression I see scales falling away and new tissue beneath. She turns herself around, holding onto me. When we sit down for the next song, she moves her chair close to mine and takes one of my hands, holding it tightly. And I realize that I've learned how to reach the Yazidis: through physical touch. *Physical touch!*

Zahra smiles. "The Yazidis like to be close to one another," she says. "They are people of peace."

"No more English," Jamal says. Moments ago he was dancing the Hokey Pokey; now he slumps into his chair, listless.

"Jamal," I say, moving to the empty chair beside him, "don't you want to learn English?"

"No, I don't think so. Not today. Maybe another day."

"Now what?" I say to Zahra.

"Will you tell us your story?" she asks the men.

Jamal, suddenly alive again, pulls up his chair in front of mine and sits so close that our knees are touching, and the others place their chairs around me, abandoning their learning.

Kodja and Eli remain on the periphery of our little circle, and once again, I don't know what to do. Leave them, or invite them in?

"Would you like to join us?" I ask.

They smile and remain seated.

"I will leave you now," Zahra says. "I have some food to make."

She kisses each woman on the cheeks and squeezes the men's hands, then leaves the room. Khifshi returns to the recliner and lies down.

I feel a little fearful, like it's all new again.

"Do you want us to tell our story now?" Jamal asks.

"Yes. Please."

"It's hard," he says. "Maybe some words, we cannot say it."

"Try. Try."

"Yazidis, they want life. They want peace. We are peace. Never we did anything bad to any people."

"What is Shingal like? Was it a happy place?" I ask.

"Yes, it was a happy place because we grew up there. We liked that life. After ISIS came, we *hate* there. We don't want to go back. Because we missed many, many people there. We lost many, many people. We don't know where they are. We don't know what happened to them. What ISIS did is they had captivity. We lost our moms and fathers and brothers. It's hard for us because we lost many, many members of our family. That's why it's hard. We never want to go back there. That's what I'm telling you. Because when you go back there, you will remember everybody in your family. For example, our cousins, we will remember we played together, we played soccer together, we played cards together, we went to school together, and we have many, many memories. Yeah, that's why it's hard."

Somehow, I feel complete belonging, despite the echoes of their stories unspoken but banging around the room, and Khifshi lying on the recliner unmoving, and the older women sitting quietly to the side. All of it violates any social decorum that I've ever known, yet it fills me—all of it fills me—and I belong to it, like blue-black darkness belongs to the full round moon.

"When did ISIS come?" I ask.

Jamal and Dakir answer in unison, their faces intent.

"August, 2014." They point to the tattoos on their arms: 03-08-14.

"You want us to tell you about the day we went to the mountains?" Jamal asks.

"Yes, please." We're at least talking in English, I think.

And Jamal and Dakir tell their story, of the day when ISIS came. They and their extended family were together in their village.

"It was a surprise. You know, on this day, August 3, 2014, ISIS came around our house. And before they came, at 9:30 o'clock, my brothers and I left for the mountains, and our family stayed. They would come behind us, after, they said. But before they left, ISIS came around our homes and they took all of our families away from us. They took them to another province, Mosul. They took 125 people. Women and children and men. We were there in the mountains seven days. After seven days, we went to

Syria, because the way between Shingal and Kurdistan, Iraq was closed at that time. ISIS blocked the way."

"What happened?"

"They sent to us a big truck from Kurdistan; we walked nine days until we got the truck. It was really hard. At that time, we didn't have food, we didn't have—because it took nine days to walk through the mountains. No food."

"What about water?"

"Yes, we had water. Every day, we had. The water was between the mountains. It's like—I don't know the name."

"A lake?"

"Yes, lake. Yes, yes. But small one."

"A stream?"

"Yes. They come from the earth. The truck took us to Syria, to Noroze refugee camp. Then after, we came back to Kurdistan, Iraq, from Syria. It took four hours, and we came back to Kurdistan."

"Why did you go back?"

"Because Syria is not our country. It was hard for us. When we came back to Kurdistan, Iraq, it was really, really hard for us. We didn't know *anything*; we didn't know any news about our families. We didn't know if they were alive or killed. Even now, even now—for example, my dad and sister, one of my brother, still, now, is in captivity by ISIS. I don't know anything about them. Maybe they are killed, maybe still in life, but I don't know anything about it."

Dakir interjects.

"You know what ISIS does with girls. You know."

"Yes," I say quietly.

"ISIS took our sisters. They will tell girls: *You have to become Muslim. If not, we will kill you. I want to get married to you. If not, I will kill you.* They took the girls. They get married to them. After that, they sell them to somebody else. And men, right away they kill. Children, they learn how to be soldiers. They teach the children bad things. Like, you have to kill someone, or like, if you see your dad, you have to kill him. They want our children to become like them. Like ISIS. That's why."

"Brainwashing? Is that the word? Brainwashing?"

"Yes, yes," Jamal says. "Brainwashing. Yes. After, like, one week, my dad, he called my brother. He found a phone, and he called my brother— he said: *We're all together. We are all still in life. But ISIS wants to separate us.* After when he hung up, my brother told us: *Everybody is still in life.* We were so happy. So happy. After that, we had complete life. We worked, because we had to work; we didn't have *nothing,* because we left everything at our village. After, like, five months, it was a little bit better than before. Because we found a job and we had money.

"At that time, my sister was with ISIS." He motions to Khifshi. "But you know why? She did like this: She's not crazy, but she pretended. That's why. She did, like, crazy; she threw things, she didn't, she didn't know anything, like, talking crazy, and ISIS saw her, and they thought maybe she was crazy."

"Do you know the story of King David?" I ask.

"No, we don't."

"Well, do you know King Solomon? He is your ancestor."

They translate among each other and speak rapidly in Kurdish.

"Yes, yes! He is our father. Our great, great, great grandfather."

"So King David—"

"Who is he?" Dakir asks.

"He is the father of King Solomon."

They talk again in Kurdish, and then a light dawns.

"Yes, yes! We know!"

I continue. "So King David is Solomon's father. And the Yazidis say that Solomon is *their* father. King David, if you read the story, he also pretended to be crazy, because he was captured. So your father—your great, great, great, great father—did the same thing as Khifshi. He was captured, and he pretended to be crazy. And the ruler said: *Ach! Get him out of here! I don't need him!*"

And I know the poignancy of talking to young men about their ancestral fathers, young men whose fathers have been murdered.

"Yes, yes! Like that," Jamal says. "Okay, I told you, after one year, my mom"—he points to Rabiya, who nods and smiles slightly— "and two of my cousins and my younger sister"—he motions to Khifshi again—"they came. Some men from Kurdistan, they have friends in ISIS—not real friends—and when a family is missing a member, they will give money to them, and they will give the money to ISIS and get the family, and tell us, come and get your family."

"He will pay a ransom," I say. "Do you know that word?"

"Yes. But if ISIS found out, they would kill everybody. But they did it at night. A guy at that time, he stole the family, and he brought them somewhere, and me and Dakir, we went with that guy, and he took the family—he gave money. Every time, like after two months, three months, someone comes back. After six months, someone comes back. All different ways. All different ways. For everybody, it's a different way."

"How did you get to Canada?"

"After three years, someone from Canadian government came to Kurdistan. And they told us: *If you want to go to Canada, we will register your name.*"

"Why didn't you want to stay in Kurdistan?" I ask. "It's your country, your culture, your people. Why did you want to come to Canada and leave everything that was familiar?"

"My answer is so clear," Jamal says. "You know why, because I lost every member in my family. That's why. You know, our country gave us bad things. They didn't give us good things."

"Kurdistan?"

"Iraq. Never they respect us, because we are Yazidis—because we are a minority, that's why. And because of our religion. The Muslim people, they want Yazidi to become Muslim. The Yazidi people like our religion. We like. That's why it's hard. Nobody wants to change their religion. It is hard. Even now, 3000 women still in captivity from ISIS. And men, children. I'm going to tell you. It was hard because we were thinking about our family. That's why we came."

"Jamal, will you tell me more about your religion and your culture?" I want to know everything about these people of peace. "Who are the Yazidi people?"

"Who are Yazidi people? I'm going to tell you who are they. You are asking me who are the Yazidi? The Yazidi people are 74 genocide. That's the Yazidi. 74 genocide. We came from genocide. Those are the Yazidi people."

I'm sick for days after the visit. Husbands killed, women and children captured by ISIS. Rescuers like miners going into the dark places of the earth, finding precious stones, and cutting them out of the rock. A well of tears is just below the surface of my skin, like coal waiting to erupt, and I can hardly move. I think about these beautiful people with so much trauma yet with laughter so effusive, so easy. In the days that follow I discover that Jamal and his family cannot hold onto any of their learning; their minds are crowded with dark, shadowy figures like the ones you see in black-and-white gangster films. I repeat the songs over and over again, but they simply do not stick, not even the simplest melodies and lyrics.

And a great darkness comes over me. After everything I learned in Israel, I'm back to square one. I recline in my Lazy-boy eating Shreddies and Cheerios, trying to determine how to *fix* this. I remember Esperance, how she simply could not learn the words—but she learned the melody. Could I do something similar with the Yazidis? Have them first learn melodies?

I go outside into the woods where I can think. Somehow, I end up at the shelter, the empty tomb where the young boy commit suicide. I kneel down and begin to compose. I begin with vowels, the most difficult sounds to master, and I sing them. And soon like the threads of so many melodies over the decades I am woven into *Pachelbel's Canon*—a canon that remained in obscurity for centuries until 1968, when Jean-Francois Paillard, musician and mathematician, reached down and pulled it out of the tomb.

But what about words? How do I teach English words? I think about how eager the Yazidis were to tell their story. Could they tell it in song, in a song with a Yazidi melody? And then it comes to me, slowly. The murals. The pride that the Eritreans felt when people watched them paint and praised their work and asked them questions. The pride of taking part in something bigger than themselves—an unfolding, and falling into conversation with spectators who perhaps, just perhaps, might see the black skin of Eritrean asylum seekers as less extreme, less *other*. I think of Jed's words about rehearsing and performance and things coming into being. But how? Where? Where would we perform? Then it dawns on me: We will perform at the New Horizons Senior Home, the dementia ward, where my father lives.

* * *

It's supper time at the ward. The residents are eating turkey breast, peas, french fries, and vanilla pudding. They are having difficulty with the peas, getting them on the fork. What a ridiculous idea to serve peas, I think. I scan the tables but don't see my father. I only see bodies, bodies backed up against some remote, impervious place, or stalled out, maybe—and backs bent over lumps of anaemic food. I'm relieved that I don't have to talk to my father. Not yet, at least.

I ask an attendant for the manager.

"I *am* the manager."

"Oh." She looks Eritrean.

"May I help you?"

"Yes. I teach English at The Booth—a resettlement centre for refugees. I'd like to—I was wondering if I could bring a few students here to sing for the people."

"I've seen you here before. Are you Walter's daughter? You look just like him."

"Yes, I am. Good memory."

"Would you like to see him? He's in his room, resting. Doesn't want to eat today."

"That's okay. I'll let him rest. So what do you think? Would it be okay if we sang here? Would the people like it?"

I look around. Would they even *know* we were here? They wouldn't remember afterwards, of course. I feel the old guilt coming up. The old guilt of consigning my father to this place; the old guilt memorializing his rapid decline once here, the dementia hunting him down like a quarry and punishing him mind and body like an army of red ants, their destruction absolute.

But did I have a choice? Regular phone calls from the police who found him wandering the streets. Incessant hand wringing and questions that drove me to *disdain* him. Falling, hitting his head. And then the anger. The anger that drove him to a wild place, a place of isolation and desolation, a hidden matrix with rules and laws of its own, existing outside the normal order of things. Too late I recognized that I had an insurrection on my hands—a man in the throes of dementia.

Did I have a choice? What a relief it was, in some ways. But the guilt, too, of passing him off to people who couldn't possibly love him like I did—the guilt of sending him to a *campos*.

"I think they would love it," the manager says. "Let's arrange it."

* * *

"I can sing," Jamal says when Zahra and I in English and Arabic make the proposal to the Yazidis in Jamal's room.

"We'll see about that," I respond.

"The older ladies—and my mom—they won't do this," Dakir says. "They don't want to learn English."

"So none of the women in class will participate?"

"I don't think so. I think just me and my brother and my sister."

"A choir of three," Zahra says.

"A chamber choir. What about you, Zahra?"

"No, no. I do not want to sing. But I will help you."

"We can't let Olga know. I'll come in the evenings."

"It will be difficult. Olga controls everything."

"Well, legally, she can't dictate what people do in their spare time."

"But she does."

"But she *can't!* Not legally!"

"She has cameras. She does not look at them, I don't think. Only if she has a reason. We have to be careful, Sarah. I need my job."

"Noted."

We stand in a circle: Zahra, Jamal, Dakir, Khifshi, and I. Rabiya sits on the bed and watches, her head tilted. We begin with Pachelbel vowels; I lead with the melody, and they follow, perfectly pronouncing the vowels and imitating the movements of English.

"Now I want you to sing your story in English," I say after a few rounds of Pachelbel. "Sing it to the tune of one of your Yazidi songs. And then—after we practice *a lot*, I think we can sing the song at the nursing home." Zahra translates. I wait for the reaction.

"No," Jamal says. "The English. I do not think it—it cannot fit our songs."

"Besides, how will you teach them?" Zahra asks. "It will be difficult. You do not understand their music. You do not know the—how do you say it?—the melodies."

"Okay. Well, can you sing your story to the tune of the *Canon*?"

"The *Canon* is much more simple. Easier to learn," Zahra says. "What do you think, Jamal?"

"We can," he says.

"Maybe we do Kurdish anthem, too," Dakir says. "Two songs."

They're right, I think. We can't impose one language on another; both will be lost. We will allow the two languages to stand, side by side, one informing the other.

The next day, Jamal, Dakir, and Khifshi record their stories on their iPhones. We sit on the bunk beds in the evening, and I transliterate their simple English sentences into Pachelbel's beautiful and haunting wedding song—and I think of Jed. His last words to me, his promise to come home before Passover. Then, he said, we will go back and forth between The Booth and the House of Refuge, together. Together, always, beginning at Passover. Passover, that feast commemorating the ancient Israelites' flight from Egyptian slavery to the Sinai desert. Passover, not just desert wandering but the forging of a *people* at Mount Sinai with a formal covenant—a certificate of marriage between HaShem and his people.

Together, the Yazidis and I and Zahra compose the song of flight—of capture and escape—and then we sing it, over and over. And the song like the stems and blossoms of a Persian carpet brings to presence the stories of flight told by tribes and tongues and nations over millennia. When we are spent from singing and our voices are hoarse, I tell them about the Eritreans' escape from slavery—the story of flight from Sinai to Israel repeated. And I tell them about the quarry, its waters still like the Dead Sea, and the flowing waters in Israel that people throw bread and pebbles into on Rosh Hashanah to cast away their sins.

Could their pain somehow be cast into the moving waters of Pachelbel, I ask them? Could the songs teach them how to *live* again—how to *live* this new life, how to stand in the pain, if only for small moments, like the moments when a pebble is cast over water and merges with the surface in a holy Eucharist before its descent into the currents? And could it be that someday, those moments might stretch into minutes or hours? And could those minutes or hours absorb the pain and like blue mountains merge with the skyline? I remind Jamal of what he tried to tell me about standing on the median between past and present, holding a balance, neither forgetting the past nor being captive to it. He nods his head, uncomprehending.

We spend months practicing the song, first learning the central melody, then perfecting pronunciation, then learning to stress the correct syllables. And then we cast it all in a Pachelbel dye, forging something new. The Yazidis will dress in their national colours, we decide: Jamal will wear red, symbolizing the blood of Yazidi martyrs; Khifshi will wear white for peace and equality; and Dakir will wear yellow to represent the source of life and light.

"Who will be the conductor?" Zhara asks.

Jamal hesitates for a moment. "You," he says. "Will you?"

"*Me*? How do I do that? I do not know how to do that."

"Just move your hands around a lot," I say. "It's easy."

"Yes. And all of us sing Canadian anthem. Not Kurdish anthem," Jamal says.

Dakir protests loudly in Kurdish. He wants to carry Kurdistan with him; Jamal wants to leave it behind. Khifshi is quiet and solemn.

"We are Yazidi—they are not. We sing Canadian anthem. All of us together."

Act One: Passover

(PESACH) — NISAN (MARCH-APRIL)

The sky is the colour of slate. Little openings expose a wall of blue behind. I sit in my Lazy-boy, curled up, twisting Jed's earring around my finger. I hear the cry of an ambulance in the distance—and then realize that it's not an ambulance; it's a wolf. A chorus begins: wolves calling to one another from every direction. Then songbirds join in, and an osprey, and finally the trumpeter swans. The quarry rounds out like an amphitheatre, and the chorus swells, pulling me into its energy field. Lakes inside of me begin to stir; colours pour out of me. And then I see in the doorway a person. Someone is there.

"Sar-ah."

It's him.

"Oh! Come in!"

He comes through the screen door, takes his shoes off. His feet are bare. He looks different. His beard. It's trimmed. And his eyes. They are patima green—but no, that's not possible. His eyes are dark like the coal mines.

I stand. I don't know what to say to him. "I—I wasn't expecting ... you're different."

He is standing barefoot in the doorway. "I'm not. I'm the same ... I'm the same today as I was yesterday. I'll be the same tomorrow." He pauses for a few moments, looks at the earring, and the seams around his eyes deepen.

* * *

We're at the New Horizons Senior Home, waiting to be buzzed into the dementia ward. Jed and I are standing close together; the Yazidis are nervously fidgeting; and Zahra is practicing wrist movements with her conductor's baton. The manager lets us in and leads us into the media room, where eight women and two men are watching television. One woman is tossing a beach ball against the wall, trying to catch it after each bounce. There are two caregivers, one watching television and the other massaging a woman's shoulders.

"They're all waiting—well, they're not *waiting*, exactly, but most of them are here," the manager says.

I scan the faces, search for my father, but he's not here. I could get him, I think, get him from his room, but the Yazidis are lining up and Zhara is wagging her baton and there's no time. Jed and I sit on the couch between two women, one wearing garish rings and bracelets, the other a broach with a yellow star, as though she knew the Yazidis were coming. She watches them closely, her eyes tracing their gestures and movements.

The Yazidis form a slender arc, Zhara stands in front and lifts her baton, and they sing. Jamal in baritone begins with a single, delicate thread, then Dakir follows, telling of the beauty of Shingal, then Khifshi comes in, harmonizing with Dakir, and together they tell the story of Khifshi's redemption—her capture, the ransom paid, and her release. And as they sing, a Shabbat spice box opens. All the aromas of Khifshi's story cling to the residents, and they become fully aware, fully alive, their past lives rushing into the present and sanding everything down, taking the rust off, giving their memories something to adhere to.

I watch Khifshi, the beautiful long lines of her scarf, her skirts, her arms. And then the timbres of her voice shift. And I see in her face the same grey wave that moved over Hannah in Israel, beginning at her eyes. It happens quickly, too quickly to respond. Her head bobs, her shoulders and chest cave in, and she falls sideways onto to the floor, cracking her head on the linoleum. She begins to scream. Loud, sharp, piercing screams. Jed is beside her in an instant, his hands under her neck, and Jamal and Dakir hold down her legs.

"Be still!" Jed says. "Be still!"

I don't know if he is addressing Khifshi or something inside of her, because his words are sharp and pressed together like the peaks of Rundle Mountain.

Khifshi arches her back and cracks her head again on the floor, and her legs go stiff and her fingers like talons begin to claw at her clothing, tearing it from her body. I try to hold her arms down, but she's too strong for me. She snaps her head from side to side like a trapped animal, shrieking and howling in a voice that is barely human.

"Be still," Jed says.

Then Khifshi goes limp. The grey recedes from her face, and Jed cradles her in his arms. "Shhh, shhh," he croons. "Shhh, shhh, shhh. You're safe, now. You're okay. Shhh, shhh. It's alright. It's alright, now." He holds her in his arms, and her tears are falling onto his feet.

"What was *that*?" I whisper.

He doesn't answer; he can only weep.

I look around the room, and the residents are watching silently, and the manager is calling 911, and the caregivers are looking on, frozen.

And then I see my father, slumped into a wheelchair. Someone has pushed him to a spot beside the television. His hands are still and he's quiet.

And my father is gone—he's gone, just like a Yazidi father. And I don't know how to pay the ransom.

* * *

Everything happens outside. I stand at the crest of the hill, and I feel the breath of HaShem. The fiddler has taken up the shofar, and the Yazidis are there, humming the Canon. Jed stands beside them, waiting for me. I go to him. Wild grasses and the colours of the quarry are soft around my feet; my temples are hot like the halves of a pomegranate. I look at Jed; his neck is like the tower of David, his hair black like a raven. He carries the fragrances of the spice box; of Kurdistan and Syria and Israel. The north wind blows, and his fragrance moves over the guests.

I go to him.

"Say my name, Sarah."

"Jed."

"Say my name."

"Jed ... Jedidiah. Jedidiah. Son of David."

"Yes. Finally, you know. You know like Eve knew Adam."

And I do—I know. Jedediah and I are *beth*. We are a Hebrew B. I am the *bayit*; Jedediah is the dot—he is the fire. *I will do a new thing*, HaShem said. *A woman will encircle a man.*

References

Agamben, Giorgio. *Means Without End: Notes on Politics*. Trans. by Vincenzo Binetti and Cesare Casarino. Minneapolis and London: Minnesota Press, 2000.

Chrismas, Lawrence. *Canmore Miners*. Calgary: Cambria Publishing, 2002.

Crawford, Glen. *Learning from Experience – A History of Development on Three Sisters Undermined Lands*. https://www.youtube.com/watch?v=JJ4B0Zb8d2Y. Retrieved 25 February, 2019.

Crawford, Glen. *A Band of Brothers – The History of Coal Mining in Canmore*. https://vimeo.com/102472475. Retrieved 25 February, 2019.

Gadamer, Hans-Georg. *Truth and Method*. Trans. by Joel Weinsheimer and Donald G. Marshall. New York: Continuum, 1997.

Hardt, Michael and Negri, Antonio. *Multitude: War and Democracy in the Age of Empire*. New York: Penguin Press, 2004.

Hotline. https://hotline.org.il/en/refugees-and-asylum-seekers-en/. Retrieved 25 February, 2019.

Ouaknin, Marc-Alain. *Mysteries of the Alphabet*. New York: Abbeville, 1999.

Quarantotto, Lucio and Sartori, Francesco. *Time to Say Goodbye*. Italy: Polydor,1996.

Stermer, Sam and Stermer, Saul. *No Place on Earth*. Magnolia Films, 2013.

Acknowledgements

Thank you to Michael Mirolla, Rafael Chimicatti, and Guernica Editions for believing in this project and bringing it into being. I've learned and grown because of you. To all of my students and refugee friends: You have enlarged my field of vision, taught me how to feel, taught me how to love. I am profoundly indebted to you. Rabbi Osadchey, thank you for enlightening me about Shabbat and the feasts. It was such a delight to sit under your teaching. Gerry Stephenson, thank you for keeping the mining stories alive. L. in Iraq and R. in Haifa, thank you for the work you do with "the least of these." You are an inspiration, changing the world one person at a time. Barbara Lamb, Jennifer Fougere, and John Robbins, thank you for sharing your craft with me. Painting, music, and teenage scientists: Does it get any better? Jeff Swart, Esther Spalding, and Mary Young, thank you for reading the manuscript, giving me ideas, and listening to my endless commentary about how to improve the book. And finally, all thanks, all praise, and all love go to HaShem, maker of Heaven and Earth.